BEN'S IN LOVE

"I'm going to the stupid homecoming dance, all right? No big deal," Nina snapped.

Claire stared at her. "Oh, no big deal. It's only about the first actual date of your life. The first dance. The first school function of any kind that you've ever willingly attended."

Nina fell silent.

"So. Who's the unfortunate guy?"

Nina took a deep breath.

"I won't laugh, I promise," Claire said. "Even if he's the biggest dork in the school. Even if it's some defenseless freshman. Or at least I'll only laugh a little."

"It's Benjamin," Nina said.

MAKING OUT #4

.Ben's in love

KATHERINE APPLEGATE

Originally published as *Boyfriends Girlfriends*

AN AVON FLARE BOOK

Grateful acknowledgment is made for the use of extended quotations from *In the Electric Mist with Confederate Dead* by James Lee Burke. Reprinted by permission of Hyperion, copyright © 1993 by James Lee Burke.

Originally published by HarperPaperbacks as *Boyfriends Girlfriends*

AVON BOOKS, INC.
1350 Avenue of the Americas
New York, New York 10019

Copyright © 1994 by Daniel Weiss Associates, Inc., and
Katherine Applegate
Published by arrangement with Daniel Weiss Associates, Inc.
Visit our website at **http://www.AvonBooks.com**
Library of Congress Catalog Card Number: 98-92783
ISBN: 0-380-80214-7

First Avon Flare Printing: September 1998

AVON FLARE TRADEMARK REG. U.S. PAT. OFF. AND IN OTHER COUNTRIES, MARCA REGISTRADA, HECHO EN U.S.A.

Printed in the U.S.A.

WCD 10 9 8 7 6 5 4 3 2 1

To Michael

Zoey Passmore

Yes, I can describe my boyfriend.

First of all, his name is Lucas Cabral. I guess he's a little taller than average, but not basketball-playing tall. Just tall enough that when we're standing up and he kisses me, I have to tilt my head back a little.

He has blond hair that tends to fall down over his eyes sometimes, which is too bad because he has these great eyes that make you get sort of wobbly when he looks at you. I mean, that's what happens to me, anyway. I don't suppose his eyes have much effect at

all on some people. Other
guys, for example.

His body? Well, he's
thin, which does not mean
he doesn't have muscles; he
does. They're just not
those bunched-up, bulky,
weight-lifting muscles like
my previous boyfriend,
Jake, had.

He has long legs, so he
probably looks great in
shorts or a bathing suit.
I'm guessing, though,
because I've never actually
seen him in either. He's
your basic Levi's kind of
guy.

I have _imagined_ him in
something other than
Levi's, though, like . . .
Never mind.

What else? Okay, he has
nice shoulders. And very
nice hands, very gentle.
Also, not that I have a lot
of guys to compare him with,

but I think he has really,
really great lips.

Really.

And that's all I can
say. At this time.

Except one more thing:
When he holds me in his
arms or kisses me, I have
this feeling that we're a
perfect fit. Do you know
what I mean? Like we were
designed especially to go
together. Now, that's really
all I can say.

Aisha Gray

Nude Descending a Staircase

It's a famous abstract painting of a woman coming down the stairs, except the artist has painted it so that it's all about motion, not about one still picture.

That's Christopher Shupe. Not nude, obviously, but always in motion. Always on his way somewhere. Sometimes he's a sort of blur, appearing, disappearing, back and forth, hello, good-bye, gotta run.

As to his actual body, it's mostly legs and when I say legs I mean all the way up to his lower back, if you see what I'm saying. Long, very muscular, very tight, on-the-move legs. If Bugs Bunny were African American (and come to think of it, are you sure he's not?), he could play the role of Christopher in a movie.

Although Christopher is much

4

more handsome than Bugs Bunny. In fact, the smallest touch from Christopher makes me start to rethink all the wise things my mother told me about not getting too involved with guys too soon.

And he kisses all the way down to your soul.

When he can stay in one place long enough.

Claire Geiger

I've had three major boyfriends in my life, so I do have some basis for comparison. First was Lucas. Yes, <u>Zoey's</u> Lucas. This was a long time ago, of course, but even then Lucas had this great sensual yet-dangerous thing going. Picture Trent Reznor only nicer, and without the tattoos.

Then there was Benjamin. Benjamin isn't someone you describe in terms of his body. Benjamin is all about intelligence and wit, although he's also major cute. It's just that you don't think of Benjamin as cute. He's too complicated to be cute.

My current boyfriend (he would not agree that's what he is, by the way) is Jake McRoyan. Yes, <u>Zoey's</u> former

6

boyfriend. What can I say? As they say at Disneyland, it's a small world after all.

Jake _is_ a person you can describe in physical terms. First of all, he's large. He's a football player and looks it. He's six two, and very muscular. Not "where's-his-neck?" muscular, just very solid, very hard. Chiseled out of marble that's warm to the touch. Very fun to look at, very fun to be close to.

He has dark, somewhat wiry hair, full lips, and gentle gray eyes that give away the fact that under the intimidating outer armor there's a very sweet guy. Nowhere in his face—or in his heart—will you find guile, or malice, or selfishness. He's the prototype of the nice guy, the loyal, duty-bound guy.

Which is why he would deny that he's my boyfriend at all.

Nina Geiger

This question is a little premature, actually. There's a chance that Benjamin Passmore will eventually become my official boyfriend. Or I'll become his official girlfriend. Or perhaps a mutual, simultaneous agreement that we are each other's boyfriend and/or girlfriend. Maybe we can get the UN to negotiate the details.

Anyway, what's he look like? It's sort of an ironic question since Benjamin's the only guy around who doesn't care much about looks. Yours, mine, his own; he couldn't care less.

He sounds enlightened, you say? Yes, he is. Also blind. Hasn't seen a thing in like seven years. He still thinks I look like a little toothpick girl with braces and no boobs. When in fact I am often mistaken for leggy supermodel Elle MacPherson.

Right.

Okay. Benjamin. Hmm. In a way everything about him is medium. Medium height, medium weight, medium-length medium-brown hair. Only when you put it all together, and especially when you add in that voice, and that sense of humor, and that whole very cool I'm-in-control thing, he's not medium anything.

I've never really had a boyfriend, but if it works out with Benjamin, it will be like I started right at the top.

One

"This isn't what you think," Christopher said.

"Not what I think. You mean that's not a very pretty girl sitting on the end of your bed?" Aisha Gray demanded. She was standing in the open doorway of his small rented room, trembling somewhere between anger and the hope that maybe, somehow, by some stretch of the imagination, it really *wasn't* what she thought. "Hello in there, by the way. My name's Aisha."

The girl inside waved back, looking embarrassed and uncomfortable. "Angela Schwegel. Uh, nice to meet you."

"She's . . . she's a friend, is all," Christopher said, pointing to the girl, his voice unusually shrill. "We were just talking."

Angela stood up, looking annoyed. She retrieved her purse and walked toward them.

Aisha waited rigidly, trying to suppress the sense of humiliation and the growing realization that the feelings already eating away at her insides were only going to get worse. She felt like she was in free fall, weightless, knowing she would inevitably hit bottom.

"Christopher, you said you didn't have a girl-friend," Angela muttered.

10

Christopher's eyes went wide, but then he tried to work up a semblance of anger. "Hey, no one ever said I couldn't see whoever I want," he said to Aisha. "Not that it was like that. Not that I'm really *seeing* Angela." Without a break, he shifted his attention to Angela. "I mean, we're not, Angela, not really. More like we were getting acquainted. Right?"

Aisha glanced at Angela. Better to know the truth, no matter how devastating. "Is that true, Angela?"

The girl hesitated only a moment. "Actually, no. We were making out. I met him at the mall a couple days ago—"

"I know," Aisha interrupted. "I was there."

"You were there?" Christopher demanded in a convincing portrayal of outrage. "You were *spying* on me?"

"He seemed like a nice guy, charming and ambitious and all," Angela said regretfully. "I like guys who have goals, you know? Most guys don't."

Aisha nodded mutely. *Yes. I was one goal. This pretty blond girl was another. Christopher has many goals.*

"Anyway. I'm out of here," Angela said, giving Christopher a disappointed shrug. She pushed past him, using the back of her hand. "I don't like guys who screw around behind their girlfriend's back, Christopher. Sorry," she said to Aisha. "I had a boyfriend like this once. My advice is lose him."

"Wait!" Christopher yelled after Angela.

"I love your hair, by the way," Aisha told the girl, for no particular reason except that none of this was Angela's fault. Aisha couldn't blame her for falling for Christopher's act. He could be very convincing. He'd convinced her, hadn't he?

Angela stopped halfway down the steps and

11

scooped the long blond ponytail over her shoulder. It fell to the middle of her behind. "Thanks, but I'm thinking of cutting it. It attracts all the wrong kinds of guys." She disappeared down the stairs, a clatter of sandals, and a moment later Aisha heard the front door of the rooming house close.

They were alone, face to face. If he would only apologize, explain that he would never deceive her again. If only he would give her some way to forgive him.

Aisha did not want to have to walk away alone.

"Now look what you did!" Christopher exploded. "I was going to . . . to do her parents' lawn. That's the only reason I was even . . . because, see, her parents have this big house with a huge garden and lawn and shrubs, and I was going to make a bid on, you know, on . . ." He seemed to run out of steam.

Aisha felt something collapse inside her. The first heat of anger was gone from her now, replaced by growing sadness that seemed to rise around her like a flood. "You know, Christopher, as lame as that lie is, there's a part of me that wants to believe it. Which is really pathetic."

"Look, Eesh, you know—" He reached to take her by the arms, but she drew back.

"No more b.s., all right? Just no more lies."

"Fine, you want to do this?" His anger was back, blazing in his eyes. "I never said I was going to be faithful to you, Aisha. I never said that, all right? Do we agree on that?"

"You never said you weren't, either."

"Okay, so I never promised you anything. So I have nothing to be ashamed of here. How could I know you were thinking it was *that* way? For all I know, *you've* been seeing other guys."

12

Aisha felt weary. They were just going through the motions now, saying things that would not affect the final outcome. Trading futile arguments that were all beside the point. "If you have nothing to be ashamed of, then why did you lie to me about going to the mall where you met that girl? And why did you just now try to lie your way out of this?"

"I didn't want to rub your face in it," Christopher said smoothly. "I mean, okay, maybe I go out with someone else; that doesn't mean I want to make a big thing out of it. It doesn't mean I don't want to be with you."

"Nice try," Aisha said flatly.

He reached for her again, and this time he was too quick. Or maybe she didn't really want to avoid his touch. Maybe she wanted Christopher to draw her to him. Maybe she wanted to feel the hardness of his chest, the muscles of his thighs against hers.

"I don't want this to mess up what we have," Christopher said. "I don't think you do, either." He bent over to kiss her. His lips were just millimeters from hers when she twisted her face away. With the palms of her hands she shoved at his chest, breaking his grip. She wasn't going to cry. At least she could salvage that much dignity.

"You lied to me, Christopher. You've been trying to get me into bed, you were trying to get that girl into bed. Probably others, too." Aisha bit her lip to keep the tears at bay for a while longer. "I'm not some number. I don't get added to some big list you keep to make yourself feel like a man."

"You have it all wrong."

"Yes. I guess I did have it all wrong. I came here today wondering whether I would tell you that I . . ." Her voice broke and she gritted her teeth, fighting to regain control. "I was going to tell you that I was in love with you. I should have known better."

"It doesn't have to end like this," Christopher said in a low, pleading voice. "We can work this out. We can still be together. I never cared about that girl or any girl the way I care about you, Eesh."

"Now, see, if I really were a romantic, that's just the kind of thing that might move me," Aisha said. "But it won't."

She turned away and marched stiffly down the stairs, hurrying to get away before the sobs overtook her.

" 'A therapist once told me that we're born alone and we die alone.

" 'It's not true.

" 'We all have an extended family, people whom we recognize as our own as soon as we see them. The people closest to me have always been marked by a peculiar difference in their makeup. They're the walking wounded, the ones to whom a psychological injury was done that they will never be able to define, the ones—' "

"Let's stop there, if you don't mind," Benjamin interrupted. He shifted on his bed, pulling a pillow from behind his back and tossing it aside.

"I thought you liked this book," Nina Geiger said. She was kicked back in his swivel chair, Doc Martens propped on the edge of his rolltop desk. She took a drink from a glass of water. Reading to Benjamin always made her thirsty.

Benjamin seemed uncharacteristically edgy. His concentration had been wavering almost since they started. It wasn't hard for Nina to guess why, and immediately she felt self-conscious. She set the pa-

14

perback down on his desk. Obviously, things weren't going to be quite as smooth as she had hoped. On the ferry ride home from school that day she had, in a moment of giddy daring, blurted out her long-hidden feelings for him. He'd responded by asking her to the homecoming dance. A couple of hours had gone by like nothing had happened, but now he must have begun to realize what he had let himself in for.

"Yeah, yeah, James Lee Burke is great; I'm just not up for anything great," Benjamin said. "I'm not up for anything I have to pay attention to. I'm . . . distracted, I guess."

"Oh."

"It's not your fault," he snapped. "I'm probably just hungry."

"It *isn't* my fault?"

"No. Well, partly. Maybe. I mean, you kind of surprised me back there on the ferry. A *good* surprise; don't get me wrong," he amended. He ran a hand through his hair and pushed the black Ray Bans up on his nose.

"You can back out if you want, Benjamin," Nina said, trying to sound nonchalant. "Feel free to bail on the whole homecoming idea." She might well have to kill him if he backed out now, the jerk, but by the same token if he was just agreeing to go out with her from some sense of pity, well, that was no good, either.

Benjamin stood up, towering over her. "I don't want to back out."

"You do, don't you?"

"No!" he nearly yelled. "No. I don't. The fact is, I'm looking forward to it. It's just unexpected. One minute we're, you know, like buds. We're Fred and Barney. Barney Rubble, not the dinosaur. Then suddenly I'm supposed to start thinking about you differently. *Very* differently. Have you told Claire?''

Nina sighed. So that was it. Claire. Her sister. What a surprise. "I haven't had time, Benjamin. You and I decided this only like two hours ago. And you know I don't talk to Claire unless it's absolutely necessary or I need her to pass the salt.''

"You want to go for a walk?" he asked suddenly.

"Should I bring the book?''

"No, let's just walk, all right? It's stuffy in here.''

"Sure," Nina said. She stood back and let him pass. Here in his own home he moved as well as a sighted person as long as things weren't relocated too much and people didn't stand in his way.

He led the way through the house to the front door. From upstairs came the sound of an outraged feminine squeal—Zoey's, of course—and a loud male laugh, presumably Lucas's.

They walked along South Street, through the tiny cobblestone-and-brick town of North Harbor, to Leeward, the road that followed the concave western coastline of Chatham Island.

"You'd better let me take your arm, if you don't mind," Benjamin said. "I can't count steps very well on Leeward. There aren't enough cross streets.''

Nina let him find her arm and they set off over the sand-blown road, past small hotels and bed-and-breakfasts, mostly boarded up now that the tourist season was over and the slow fall season was well under way. The ocean crashed with gentle insistence on the beach, depositing green-black wreaths of seaweed and sending shorebirds skittering stiff-legged away from the surf. The sun was setting across the water behind the mainland city of Weymouth, blanking out the detail of the ten-story bank and insurance buildings,

16

turning them into black building blocks piled before a red-and-orange backdrop.

"How's it look?"

"Nice sunset," Nina said.

"Yeah?"

"A lot of orange and some pink. The clouds look like they're burning at the edges, you know what I mean?"

"I remember," he said in a softer tone. "Nice image, though. Thanks."

They walked on in silence. Nina knew he liked long periods when he could just listen to all the sounds she barely noticed, and smell the salt and the pine and the mouthwatering smoke of barbecues from the homes set back off the road.

"Sorry I got all tense on you," he said after a while.

"I understand. I mean, you're a nice person and you know I've been going through some bad stuff in my own life. So, really, it was sweet of you to ask me to the dance and all. I mean, I know you don't feel, you know . . . You know, like *that*."

"Oh, shut up, Nina." He said it gently. "You don't know what I feel. I don't even know what I feel."

"Sure I do. You still have it bad for Claire. I don't understand why—I think you're too nice for her. I think my sister is so cold she can poop ice cubes when she wants to, but if you're all in love with her . . ." She shrugged, unable to go on. Two hours of quiet pleasure had turned to dust. But at the same time, there was a feeling of relief. She wouldn't have to worry about whether she could deal with it or whether the internal demons of memory would ruin it all.

Benjamin grinned. "Poop ice cubes?" He laughed gleefully. "Now *that's* an image."

"I have the actual photographs of her doing it. I'd show them to you, only you can't see." Nina noticed a shape approaching rapidly from the south. "Hey, it's Aisha."

Aisha rode up on her bike, her explosion of springy black curls planed and reshaped by the ocean breeze. At first she seemed reluctant to stop, but then she pulled over. "Hi, Nina, hi, Ben."

"What's up, Eesh?" Nina asked.

"Nothing. Nothing. Well, I better get going. Um, is Zoey home?"

"She was when we left," Benjamin said.

"Okay, bye," Aisha said quickly. She got her bike going and rode swiftly away.

"What's with her?" Nina wondered.

"Christopher lives down that road, doesn't he?"

"Aha. You're right. Possible trouble. She looked kind of spacey." Nina dug in her purse and found her pack of Lucky Strikes.

"Are you sucking on one of your unlit cigarettes?"

"No," Nina lied, sticking a cigarette in her mouth.

"I can smell it."

"Must be the ocean."

"Uh-huh. Look, Nina. Of course I've thought about you," Benjamin said, plowing back into their conversation with jarring suddenness.

Nina raised an eyebrow. "Thought about me? What does that mean?"

"I mean," he said in an exaggeratedly patient voice, "that I know you use a shampoo that smells like coconuts, and that you occasionally wear a perfume that smells like vanilla, and another that smells like melon. Which probably explains why I often get hungry when you're around.

"And, of course I know that sometimes you're si-

18

lently cussing me out and giving me the finger because you're mad at me. I also know you are a basically cool person. Plenty of free-floating hostility, plenty of strangeness, but no meanness. I know that you have soft fingers, and that you have . . . well, never mind. The point is, it's not like I've never thought about you. In *that* way. I mean, you are a girl, and I am a guy, and we do spend a lot of time together."

Nina nodded, not trusting her voice to respond.

"Don't nod. How the hell am I supposed to know if you're nodding? All I'm trying to say is . . . I don't know what I'm trying to say. I want to be straight with you because whatever else you are, you're my friend, okay?"

"Uh-huh," Nina managed to mutter.

Benjamin stopped and turned toward her. He aimed his sunglasses at her, as always just a little off-target, but close enough to almost make her believe he could see her and that he was looking into her eyes. "I'm in love with Claire. It's fading, and maybe it will more over time. I don't know. I know I like you. A lot. And maybe that will change into something more. That's all I have to say. I don't want to b.s. you, Nina, or make promises. Except I'll make the promise that one way or the other, I'll always be your friend."

Nina took a deep, shaky breath. So he *was* still in love with Claire, which was no surprise at all.

On the other hand, Benjamin had admitted that the thought of Nina as an actual *female* had occurred to him once or twice. "I want you to know what you're getting into with me, Nina, that's all. And now, if *you* want to change *your* mind about this weekend, I'll understand."

Nina chewed on her lower lip. It would be about a

million times easier just to stay home from the game on Friday, and a billion times easier to skip the homecoming dance on Saturday. Weymouth High was a fairly small school. And by now everyone there, from cheerleaders to jocks to brains to the glue-huffing morons in detention, knew that she had accused her uncle of molesting her. Everyone was busy nodding and saying things like, *Wow, all this time I thought she was a lezzie and now it turns out she was just screwed up about guys*. And showing up at homecoming with Benjamin, whom half the girls in school had their sights on, would be like pouring gasoline on the gossip fire.

A very large number of girls, including, possibly, Claire, would be pissed. So at least there was something positive.

"Nah. I can't dump you, Benjamin," Nina said. "People would feel sorry for you, sitting home all alone."

Benjamin smiled. "So what are you going to wear?"

"Like you would know the difference?"

"I didn't mean clothing. I meant I like the vanilla stuff better."

"Ow, ow. That hurts." Zoey Passmore winced and tried to pull away.

"That's what you get for throwing things at me without warming up first," Lucas said, unimpressed by her complaints. "You've pulled your shoulder muscle. If you're going to heave a book at my head, you should at least warm up—you know, stretch. All that time going out with a jock and you learned nothing." He poured some more oil into his palms, rubbed them together, and went back to work kneading Zoey's bare shoulder.

Lucas was leaning against the mountain of pillows at the head of Zoey's bed. She sat cross-legged with her back to him, T-shirt off and the shoulder strap of her bra lowered.

"I didn't heave a *book* at your *head* in a *jealous rage*," Zoey corrected him in a drowsy, relaxed voice. "Oh, that's good; yeah, yeah, like that. I just *tossed* a *magazine* to you."

"A very big magazine. Very fast toss."

"Do that some more. It's your fault, anyway. You asked for it."

"I was just quoting from the magazine," Lucas said mildly. "I didn't make up the statistics. I was just pointing out that in the article they said the majority of people our age are having sex. I didn't necessarily mean anything by it."

Zoey twisted her head toward the good side, pried open one eye, and gave him a look. He broke into a smile. "Okay, maybe I had a small ulterior motive."

"Yeah, *maybe*," Zoey said dryly. "See, your mistake was you shouldn't have gone right from talking about that to talking about Louise Kronenberger."

"I was making a joke. I was just saying she probably accounted for a lot of that statistic all by herself. Joke. Ha ha."

"Ow, not quite that hard," Zoey said.

"You should put some ice on it," Lucas said.

Zoey twisted around again. "So should you."

"Oh, that's funny, Zoey."

"Anyway, if you like K‑burger so much, you'll have the perfect opportunity to get to know her," Zoey said with poisoned sweetness. "You have the big ceremonial homecoming king and queen dance.

21

Maybe you could bring a copy of that magazine article. You could whisper statistics in her ear.''

Lucas sighed deeply. ''This is why I didn't want to get into the whole homecoming thing. I'm getting swept up into the whole school-spirit-popular-people-who-saw-who-with-who-else thing.''

''You're trying to change the subject,'' Zoey said.

Lucas suddenly pulled her onto her back and crouched over her, pinning her arms over her head. ''No, *now* I'm changing the subject.''

He lowered his face to hers and they kissed, a long, slow kiss that left them both breathless.

Suddenly there was a knock at the bedroom door. And before Zoey could think of how to respond, the door opened.

''Aisha!'' Zoey gasped. She pushed Lucas off her and began a frantic search for her shirt. Lucas grabbed a pillow and rested it on his lap.

''Oh, God, I'm interrupting something, aren't I?'' Aisha said.

''No, no,'' Zoey said shrilly, leaning over the side of the bed to rummage beneath it. She came up with the T-shirt, untwisted it, and pulled it on over her head. ''Come in, Eesh,'' she said. ''We were just, uh . . .'' Zoey looked helplessly at Lucas.

''We were discussing, um, statistics,'' Lucas said, sending Zoey a disgruntled glare.

''I just broke up with Christopher,'' Aisha blurted.

Zoey shoved a tumble of wispy blond hair out of her eyes and looked at her friend more closely. Aisha's dark eyes were puffy and outlined in red. It was a startling realization—Aisha had been crying.

''What happened?'' Zoey asked, pushing Lucas away to make room on the bed for Aisha to sit beside her.

"This sounds like girl stuff," Lucas said. "I think I'll just head on out." He climbed off the bed and started toward the door.

"I caught him with some girl in his room," Aisha said bleakly.

"A girl? In his room?" Zoey was stunned. But not so stunned that she didn't notice the way Lucas seemed to cringe at this news.

"Bye," Lucas said, slipping out and closing the door behind him. "I'll go home and try that ice idea."

"Well, were they just talking, or what?" Zoey asked, waving a distracted good-bye to Lucas. She put her arm around Aisha's shoulders.

"They were . . . they were, well, not quite like you and Lucas just were, but close."

"He was just giving me a shoulder rub," Zoey said, blushing a little.

"The girl said they were making out."

"The girl?"

"The girl from the mall."

"The girl from . . . *That* girl? The girl with the hair?"

"She was really pretty nice," Aisha said.

"Pretty nice? She was making out with your boyfriend, wasn't she?"

"She didn't know. Christopher told her he didn't—" She had to stop and fight back a sob. "He told her he didn't have a girlfriend." She ended on a fierce note, her eyes blazing. "And now he doesn't, the rotten, stinking slug."

"I'm really sorry, Eesh."

"I'm not," Aisha said bitterly. "I've just relearned my lesson. See, it's my fault. I always said if you get too into one guy, he'll always dump on you sooner or later. Guys. They're all pigs."

"They're mostly pigs," Zoey agreed reasonably.

"*All* of them," Aisha insisted. "They only want one thing. You'll find out someday. Not that I can say *I told you so*. Not anymore." She wiped away a tear that had trickled down her cheek.

Zoey glanced at the door to her bedroom. She should be telling Aisha that she was wrong. Some guys weren't like that. Some guys could be counted on no matter what.

Two

Nina sat on the living room couch, legs stretched out along its length, a notebook open on her lap, a bag of Doritos, a bowl of salsa, and a root beer on the coffee table within easy reach. A stubby, unlit Lucky Strike hung from the corner of her mouth. She had to strain to see what she was writing in the notebook because the only light came from the muted television. She scooped up some salsa and popped the chip in her mouth. Then she wrote:

5. Pee is blue.

She took a swig from the sweating can of root beer. Who decided this? Why not green? Why not purple? Why blue?

"What's on?"

Nina jerked and bit her tongue. She glared up at her sister. "Jeez, Claire. You creep around here like Morticia."

"What do you want me to do? Ring a little bell so you'll know I'm coming?" Claire sat down in the wing-backed easy chair. She was wearing a silk robe and had her hair wrapped in a damp towel.

"Actually, that's not a bad idea," Nina said. "Would you mind?"

"What's on?" Claire asked again. Then she wrinkled her nose. "Hot sauce? Right before you go to bed?"

"I'm not going right to bed. I have this homework to do first. I'm going to stay up and watch Dave."

"You'll be in a coma all day tomorrow," Claire observed. "Nothing unusual about that, though, I guess. What's the homework?"

"Modern Media," Nina said. "We're supposed to list some of the hidden messages beneath the surface of commercials." She laughed. "My kind of class—watch TV, get a grade. I was so right to go with this instead of a lit. elective. Those poor suckers are all reading Faulkner. I'm observing that pee is blue."

"Excuse me?"

"TV pee. It's blue. You know, baby diapers, old people diapers, the 'liquid' is always blue. Why blue? Why not green or red? These are the big questions I'm dealing with here. I feel I'm on the cutting edge of human knowledge."

"Red would look like blood," Claire pointed out. "Red pee?"

"You're right. That would be like, *Hey, use our Depend Undergarments and pee blood.*" Nina nodded approvingly. "Thanks for clearing that up. It's so helpful having an all-knowing senior right here in the house with me."

"I don't know if that's exactly what your teacher had in mind," Claire said. "Let me have a drink of your soda."

"Here." Nina leaned forward as far as she could, just barely able to hand the can to Claire.

"What else do you have?"

Nina held her notebook sideways to read by the flickering blue-gray light of the television. "Well, first of all, I noticed that anytime you have a married couple in a commercial, the woman is always smarter, younger, and better looking than the man."

"Now, see, *that's* a good observation," Claire said.

"Um, and, wait, I can't read . . . Oh, yeah. That ad for the company that makes bulletproof vests? They say, *Every year schmuh police officers are killed.*"

"Schmuh?"

"Exactly. Instead of saying a number, they just say *schmuh* and hope no one will notice."

"Okay."

"Seriously," Nina insisted.

"Okay."

"Then I noted that it's okay to show animated earwax exploding out of your ear, but you never see a laxative commercial where—"

"I get the idea," Claire interrupted quickly.

"Then I noticed that girls who have their period always wear white. Which led to the question of blue body fluids."

"You'll be Mr. Mifflin's star student," Claire said dryly. She stood up, bent at the waist, and began unwrapping the towel, letting her long damp hair hang down. She stood up quickly and began fluffing it dry with her fingers. "I'm getting my ends trimmed tomorrow at the mall, so I'll have the car." She made a wry face. "I was going to shop for a dress for the homecoming dance, but as of right now I don't exactly have a date."

"You still haven't brought Jake to his knees yet? Huh. I'm starting to have a better opinion of old *Joke.*"

"I may just have to stay home with you," Claire said.

Nina started to answer but stopped herself. Sooner or later Claire would find out, and it wasn't like Nina was doing anything wrong. Still. It was sort of two major announcements in one—first, she had to make the big announcement that actually, surprising as it seemed, she *was* going to homecoming. This by itself would be an event as rare as a major earthquake. Second, there was the matter of *whom* she was going to the dance with.

"I said . . . I said I may just have to stay home with you," Claire repeated. She was eyeing Nina closely from beneath a questioning brow.

"Uh-huh," Nina said, pretending to be absorbed by her notebook.

"Don't *uh-huh* me, Nina. I know you. What are you not telling me?"

Nina shrugged.

"Spill."

"I don't have to tell you everything, Claire."

"Yes, but you're going to anyway, so since it's late and I have to go dry my hair, why not just cough it up now and get it over with?"

"Going to the dance," Nina mumbled under her breath, pretending to be absorbed by the TV screen.

Claire sighed. "What would that be if you were speaking English?"

Nina rolled her eyes. "I'm going to the stupid homecoming dance, all right? No big deal."

Claire stared at her. "Oh, no big deal. It's only about the first actual date of your life. The first dance. The first school function of any kind that you've ever willingly attended. Is this because of the whole thing with Uncle Mark? Are you, you know—"

"Am I becoming psychologically unhinged?"

"You were born psychologically unhinged," Claire said.

Nina fell silent. The mention of her uncle had cast a pall over her. This was how it would be from now on. Everyone, even Claire, would see everything she did in the light of terrible events that had happened a long time ago.

"Sorry," Claire said, downcast. "That was over the line." Then she smiled her rare, wintry Claire smile. "Not the part about you being psychologically unhinged. That's just a fact. But I won't bring up that creep's name again."

"Cool," Nina said.

"So. Who's the unfortunate guy?"

Nina took a deep breath.

"I won't laugh, I promise. Even if he's the biggest dork in school. Even if it's some defenseless freshman. Or at least I'll only laugh a little."

"It's Benjamin," Nina said.

Claire froze. For a full minute she didn't say anything. "Oh."

"Look, *you're* not going out with him anymore," Nina said defensively.

"No, I'm not."

"This isn't going to, like, you know . . . is it?"

"I always knew you had a crush on him," Claire said a little sadly.

"We're just friends. I think."

"It's not any of my business," Claire said. Her lips were narrowed to the point of disappearing.

Nina gritted her teeth. This was actually more awkward than she had expected it to be, and she'd expected it to be pretty awkward. She squeezed the ends of her cigarette between her fingers and peeked up at her sister.

"Well, I have to go finish drying my hair," Claire said with sudden, determined brightness.

"Yeah. See you tomorrow morning."

"Uh-huh."

"Good night!" Nina yelled after her sister. If there was an answer, she didn't hear it.

Nina and Benjamin. *Nina* and Benjamin. Nina and *Benjamin*.

Her sister and her former boyfriend. Her very recently *former* boyfriend.

Claire finished running the hair dryer over the ends of her hair and hung the dryer back on its hook beside the medicine cabinet. She began combing while searching her face for any blemishes. As usual, she found none.

Of course Nina had a crush on Benjamin; Claire had known that for a long time. But lots of people had crushes on lots of other people. People didn't usually act on their crushes.

Especially Nina.

Claire turned off the bathroom light and climbed the stairs to her bedroom. It was on the top level of the house, the only room on the third floor. Her bed was neatly made, her clothing put away. The lighting was soft—shaded lamps with pink bulbs. On her desk was a box that kept track of the barometric pressure, wind speed, and temperature outside. On a wall she had a large, National Geographic map of Antarctica.

Attached to one wall was a steel ladder that led to a square hatch in the ceiling. She climbed the ladder, graceful from long experience, pushed open the hatch door, and emerged into the chill air of the widow's

30

walk, a section of flat roof covered in weathered wood and surrounded by a waist-high railing.

It was Claire's place, even more than her room was. No one else ever came up here—not Nina, not Claire's friends. From here on a clear day or night, she could see all of North Harbor, Chatham Island's tiny village. She could see the few streetlights shining silver on cobblestoned streets, the occasional porch light piercing the dark shadow of the hill that rose from the southern edge of the town. She could look across the water to Weymouth, the mainland city four miles away that glittered bright and cold, moonlight on glass-walled buildings.

To the north, past the slow sweep of the lighthouse's beacon, and to the east, only empty ocean— a vast, dark force that gently massaged the rocks and beaches of Chatham Island and could, on occasion, attack the island as if it were trying to sink it once and for all.

The breeze was too cool, sneaking under and through her robe. It raised goose bumps and reminded her that the full, brutal Maine winter was not so far off.

Benjamin had never come up to the widow's walk, but he had asked her, from time to time, to describe for him what she saw from here. And in the process of telling him she had realized how few details she had ever really noticed. By the end of their relationship she had learned to see much more clearly.

Well, if Nina was ready to take the plunge into dating, then Benjamin would be a good person for her to be with. He was smart and patient and understanding. He knew what had happened between Nina and that bastard Uncle Mark. He had been there when

Nina had finally, after so many years of shamed silence, leveled the accusation.

Yes, if Nina was going to start dating, then Benjamin was a good choice.

It just seemed a little strange. Claire and Benjamin had done everything together. Almost everything. Everything *but*. Now, he would be going out with her own sister. It was an unnerving thought.

Claire pulled the robe tighter around her. She wished she'd at least worn some socks. Still, she was reluctant to leave her aerie just yet. In warmer weather she often slept up here. During storms she liked to huddle under her slicker and watch the lightning snap the surface of the water.

When she had broken up with Benjamin, he'd said something to her . . . something about her being isolated . . .

She went to the tall brick chimney that fronted one end of the widow's walk. She reached around to locate the loose brick and pried it out. Inside the cavity was her diary. She took it out, sat down, and began riffling back through the pages. She'd written down what Benjamin had said. Yes, there it was, as she remembered it.

"You're an isolated, lonely, superior person, Claire. You sit up there on your widow's walk and watch the clouds overhead and the little people down below. And they have to be below you,

32

that's the important thing, because you
can't tolerate an equal for long."

She smiled as she read it. Benjamin always did
have a way with words.
Nina and Benjamin.
Claire pulled the pen from the spine of the diary.

Monday, 11:30 p.m. The wind is out
of the southwest at about seven or eight
knots. The temperature

She squinted to read the mercury on the thermom-
eter nailed to the railing.

is 59 degrees.

No wonder she was cold.

Nina is going with Benjamin to
homecoming.
As things stand right now, I don't
have a date. I see very little chance that
Jake will suddenly change his mind.
I've done everything I can think of to
get him to

33

To what? To love her? He already loved her. To want her? Oh, he wanted her badly enough. That wasn't the problem.

forgive me.
To stop blaming me for things that happened years ago.

That's what stood between them. *All* that stood between them. His guilt over loving the girl who had been responsible for his brother's death. And now that guilt was corroding his life. He had been drinking. Drinking at the wrong times and in the wrong circumstances. He had narrowly avoided missing his last football game.

I gave up Benjamin for Jake. I felt threatened by the way Benjamin kept trying to force the truth from me. But now the truth is out.
I love Jake. But how long can I stand his rejection?

The breeze carried the melancholy, muffled clang of some distant buoy. Far, far out to sea, the faint lights of ships traveled south along the horizon.

Sometimes I wish everything would just go back to the way it was before. Jake with Zoey. Me with Benjamin.

Only now, Zoey was with Lucas. Nina might be with Benjamin.

And Claire?

Claire was isolated, lonely, perhaps even superior, on her widow's walk.

The only real images I have of either
Claire or Nina are from years ago,
back before I lost my sight. I ~~remeber~~
remember Claire's hair, which was
long then, just like it is now. I remember that it was dark, maybe even
black. And I remember an expression
she wore, even as an eleven-year-old, a
cool, appraising look, like everyone
around her had to prove themselves to
her satisfaction, and she wasn't going
to be easy to impress.

Nina's a year younger, and I remember her as less grown-up looking than
Claire. She had braces, and a cocky
look that was sort of a better-natured,
more mocking version of Claire's.

But I've had no visual input to up-
date either picture, so those old images
persist when I deal with these two
girls, although I've added many, many
details—the plush softness of Claire's
lips, the heavy silk of her hair, the
smooth skin of her legs, ~~hte~~ the heat I
could always feel long before I touched
her, the way she smells somehow of
moonlight and ocean breezes. I think I
will always know the beat of her heart,

the cool precision of her voice, her laughter, so infrequent that when it came, it always shocked me.

And yes, I know she's calculating and self-serving and even ruthless when she feels she has to be. I know she's impatient with anyone less gifted than herself, that she exploits the insecurities she brings out in other people.

But I also know that underneath it all, sometimes *way* underneath it all, Claire is a decent human being, striving to figure out what's right and to do it. I now know that if I were ever in trouble, tomorrow or ten years from now, I could count on Claire to help. Of course, she'd bitch about it a little first.

Nina? I have less of Nina. A very old image joined to new information that, brought together in my mind, still doesn't form a complete picture.

No one is faster with a deadly accurate slam. And no one is so careful never to really cause pain. She's bold and provocative and individualistic, but she's also shy and and awkward and insecure. I think of her as a person who can blush in terrible mortification or laugh defiantly. There's no one I'd rather just hang out with, listen to TV with, walk with.

But Nina as something more than a friend? I don't know. That concept hasn't taken hold for me. I know it's strange, but in a way I can't picture Nina as having a body. Legs, arms, shoulders, lips, breasts. I think of her as an attitude, a sense of humor, a lightning-quick jab that makes me laugh.

But as someone I might hold? Sa As someone I might touch and kiss? I don't know that Nina.

Not yet.

Three

The clock over the chalkboard jerked the final minute and the bell rang. Zoey all but ran for the exit, snatching up her books and banging her leg on the desk in her hurry. She was one of the first people into the hallway, though hundreds boiled out behind her and from all the doors lining both sides of the stuffy, over-lit hall.

"I have no idea what that woman is trying to teach me," she muttered under her breath. A freshman guy paused to look at her curiously. "Don't ever take trig, that's my advice," she told him. "In fact, just drop out now."

The second and third periods of the day were her least favorite. First period was fine. Journalism. No problem. After lunch everything was fine, too, with American lit., history, and French. But second period was trigonometry and it was followed immediately by gym. She didn't understand trig—she would never, ever, if she lived a thousand years, understand trig. Her brother and Claire and Aisha all laughed at her for being a mathematical idiot. The three of them took calculus, the creeps.

As for gym, well, that had just been stupidity on her part. She, Claire, and Aisha had all brilliantly decided to put off the junior-year gym requirement and take more exciting electives. Now they were among the very few senior girls still forced to make fools of themselves throwing basketballs blindly toward a backboard that she, at least, never hit; bouncing from trampolines; and, in Coach Anders's latest annoying brainstorm, playing tennis. The tennis had to be played outside, which would be even less fun when the temperature dropped to minus five and the wind blew through at fifty miles per hour. To make matters worse, the only other senior girls taking gym were on their way to becoming phys-ed majors. These girls enjoyed bouncing tennis balls off Zoey's head while she flailed away clumsily with her racket.

"One more year of this place," she muttered.

Then four years of college.

She sighed and headed down the hall, down the stairs, and down the lower-floor hall, heading on unwilling feet toward the gym.

A hand shot out from a crush of kids and grabbed her arm. Lucas twirled her to face him and put his arms around her. "What, you can't even stop and say hi?"

"Hi. I didn't see you," Zoey said. She kissed him lightly, and he pulled them both to an unoccupied few inches of locker-lined wall. They kissed with more concentration, far away for a few moments from the echoing shouts and slamming metal locker doors all around them.

"Now I'm in a much better mood," Zoey said, leaning against him. "Your hair's wet."

"Just got out of gym. Were you in a bad mood?"

"I'm always in a bad mood after trig. I don't personally believe there should be classes where nothing can be explained in English and it all relies on numbers and signs. Besides, when in my life am I ever going to have to deal with cosines, tangents, or any of that stuff?''

"You might have to cosign a loan. Or is that getting off on a tangent?''

Zoey groaned and made a face. "That's the kind of thing I expect from Nina.''

Lucas kissed her again. And again, trigonometry, gym, and pretty much the entire rest of the world ceased to exist.

"Is that more the kind of thing you expect from me?'' Lucas asked huskily.

"Mmm.''

"Let's bail. We'll sneak off, get your folks' car out of the garage, cruise down to Portland or even to Boston. Have fun. What can they do to me? I'm the newly elected homecoming king. I am all-powerful.''

"Don't tempt me when I'm on the way to gym class,'' Zoey said.

"Oh, I think you look cute in your little shorts.''

"When have you seen me in my gym outfit?''

"I'm in algebra for the mathematically impaired on the third floor then,'' he said. "Perfect view of the field. The guys especially like it when the girls stretch out—you know, bending over to grab your ankles and all that. I'm trying to figure out how to smuggle binoculars into class.''

"It must be nice having a one-track mind. So few outside distractions.''

Lucas laughed. "It beats paying attention to algebra.''

"I better get going; Coach Anders makes you run laps if you're late. Bye, I'm off to shower with strangers.''

"I'll trade you. I'll go shower with the girls, you can do my algebra."

"On top of trig? I'd rather have my hair pulled out, one hair at a time."

"Hi, Lucas." Pause. "Oh, and hi, Zoey."

"Hey, Louise," Lucas said with careful nonchalance.

"Hi, Louise," Zoey said. Louise Kronenberger was wearing bell-bottomed jeans with a tight, loose-knit sweater over no bra. Lucas's eyes were darting down to peer between the mesh.

"Hey, homecoming king," Louise said. "We need to get together and talk about Friday and Saturday."

"We do?" Lucas asked. He shot an alarmed glance toward Zoey.

"We have a couple of official duties," Louise said.

"I thought all we had to do was look surprised when they announce we won, and then dance."

The actual announcement of the homecoming queen and king would come at halftime in the game, but for the last two years the administration had always leaked the results early. The precaution was thanks to an earlier homecoming queen who hadn't expected to win and had showed up tripping on LSD. She had become terrified of the opposing team's mascot and run screaming from the field.

"We want to look good for the dance, right?" Louise said.

The warning bell rang. A collective groan went up from the masses and people began disappearing back into classrooms.

"I don't care how I look, Louise," Lucas said. "I'd wear a bag over my head if I thought I could get away with it."

"I have to get going," Zoey said.

"Me too," Lucas said.

"Which way are you going?" Louise asked Lucas.

"Uh, third floor."

"Me too." Louise grinned. "We can talk on the way. Bye, Zoey." She took Lucas's arm and began towing him along. Lucas looked back over his shoulder and sent Zoey a helpless look.

Zoey made a face and silently mouthed a single descriptive word in reference to Louise Kronenberger.

Lucas grinned. But he still followed Louise up the stairs.

"My towel's all gross," Zoey complained, wrinkling her nose at the dank smell. It actually smelled even worse than the rest of the locker room. She threw the towel into her open gym locker on top of sneakers, deodorant, shampoo, and an uneaten Snickers bar that had been in there since the first day of school. "Will someone remind me to take it home and wash it? Now what am I going to do? I'm wet, but if I use that rag, I'll smell like dirty socks all day."

"Don't look at me," Aisha said, raising her arms to let her shirt settle down over her. "You can't borrow *my* towel. Hey, do you believe Christopher? That walking hormone. No apology, nothing. Just hands out the rackets and balls like he doesn't even know who I am."

One of Christopher's many jobs included working part-time as equipment manager for the gym department.

"I was not going to ask for your towel, Aisha," Zoey protested. "Gross. Borrowing someone else's used towel?" She looked around distractedly. The truth was, she'd have gladly borrowed Aisha's towel. She glanced at Claire, doing her makeup, but Claire

43

was ignoring her helpless look. "What did you want Christopher to do?" she asked Aisha, feeling cranky. "He was working, and Coach was right there the whole time. Besides, Eesh, I thought you'd already forgotten Christopher existed. Damn, I cannot put clothes on over wet skin—they'll cling."

"Cling to what?" Claire muttered, concentrating on her eyeliner.

"I don't really care what Christopher does anymore," Aisha said. "I was just saying that on top of everything else, he was rude."

"I'm freezing here," Zoey said, "and all I get is clever remarks and indifference."

Claire began methodically pulling paper towels from the dispenser on the tiled wall beside the sinks. "Here." She handed the wad to Zoey and returned to leaning over the sink to put on blush.

Zoey began applying the paper towels to various parts of her body. They stuck, making her look sort of like a shingled roof. Aisha tilted her head at a critical angle and looked Zoey over. "I think you may have a look going there, Zo. Let's take a picture and send it to *Glamour*. I see it as a continuation of the 'waif look.' "

"Zoey *is* the waif look," Claire said. "Or would be if she could look just a little dumber. You need to work on the blank, uncomprehending stare, Zoey, if you're going to go for that true Kate Moss thing. You already have the body."

Zoey sent Aisha a conspiratorial smile. "It's terrible when the wheels of fashion turn against you full-figured gals, isn't it, Claire?" Zoey teased. "Your little snide remarks don't bother me, not anymore. The whole world now sees that small is beautiful. This is my hour. Juglessness rules. The unbuffered

44

shall inherit the earth. Flat is powerful.''

"You're covered in wet paper towels, oh powerful one,'' Claire pointed out.

"New from *The Limited*—the wet paper towel bodysuit,'' Zoey said. She began peeling them off and slipped into her clothes, grimacing at the residual clamminess.

"That's another thing about Christopher,'' Aisha said, back to fuming. "He once told me I had big feet. But have you seen his forehead? No, because he *has* no forehead.''

"I saw K-berger and Lucas having a very close conversation up in the third-floor hallway,'' Claire said, not even bothering to conceal the sly look in her eyes. "They look like a good couple to be homecoming . . . whatevers. Now, K-berger, there's a girl who will never be able to pull off the waif look.''

"Homecoming is stupid,'' Aisha said. She fluffed her hair with both hands. It sprang out in a voluminous, curly mass that Zoey greatly admired. "What's it even mean? Homecoming?''

"That's what all the girls say who don't have a date,'' Claire said dryly. "And this year, I agree with you—homecoming *is* stupid.''

Zoey's jaw dropped. "You don't have a date? No wonder you're being so snippy. I assumed it was just PMS.''

"Don't pick on Claire because she doesn't have a date,'' Aisha grumbled. "Two out of the three girls standing here don't have a date for homecoming. In fact, Zoey, you seem to be in the minority. Although personally I'm glad. I hate football games and I hate dances. I'd rather stay home and watch . . . whatever's on Friday and Saturday night.''

"*20/20* on Friday,'' Claire said. She finished her

45

makeup, and Zoey took her place at the sink. "Barbara Walters. I think she's interviewing some politician. Huge fun. Maybe we could watch it together. But if you do stay home, Aisha, Christopher will laugh and think you couldn't get any other guy."

Aisha's eyes narrowed. "You know, you're right."

"How would he even know?" Zoey reasoned. She snatched Claire's blush. "He's not in school except to work. He would only go to the dance if you invited him, Aisha."

"Oh, he'll find out somehow," Aisha said through gritted teeth. "Claire's right. He'll think he's such hot stuff that without him all I can do is sit at home and watch *20/20*."

"*SNL*'s on Saturday night," Claire added. "For whatever that's worth. Not much, usually."

"What are you going to do?" Zoey asked Aisha. "You don't have any guys on hold or anything."

"I can get a date," Aisha said defensively. "Hey. How about Benjamin?" She shot Claire a *so there* look.

Claire shook her head. "He's taking Nina."

"Excuse me?" Zoey said, her eyes wide. "Benjamin is taking Nina? My brother, Benjamin, is taking out Nina, one of my best friends, and I don't know about it?"

"Nina probably thinks you'll make a big deal out of it," Claire said. "And you know Benjamin. Not exactly Mister Gossip."

"I'm his only *sister*," Zoey nearly yelled.

"Nina just told me last night," Claire said. "You know how she is about guy stuff."

"Yeah, I do know." Zoey's face turned serious. "By the way, have they arrested that creep uncle of yours yet?"

"It's complicated." Claire sighed. "Maine laws, Minnesota laws. My dad has a lawyer working on it."

"Great. So Nina suddenly emerges from the nunnery and instantly steals the only remaining guy around," Aisha said. "Now what am I going to do for a date?"

"Maybe Nina will trade you straight across," Claire suggested. "Benjamin for Christopher. Throw in some cash and I think she might consider it."

"Very funny," Aisha said. "But I don't need your pity. I'll probably have a date by the end of the day. One that will make Christopher eat his liver."

"Not that you care what he thinks," Zoey added.

Four

Lucas decided against lunch in the cafeteria. The food was lousy and he didn't feel comfortable eating with Zoey. Zoey, Aisha, and Nina had made a long-standing ritual of having lunch together—no guys, no outsiders, with the occasional exception of Claire. Zoey had told him he was welcome, but when he was there the conversation tended to die out, and he'd gotten the message—lunchtime was girl time.

He left the campus and headed toward the nearby Burger King. He had a little money now from doing some work on his father's lobster boat. He'd been mucking out the bilges, which was about as nasty a job as you could find anywhere, and doing some painting, which wasn't so bad. His father might be a son of a bitch, but he paid a fair wage for the work. A Whopper and fries wouldn't set him back too much.

The Burger King was filled with other kids from school, competing for space with business-women from the nearby office buildings and guys from a road crew that was repaving a section of the street.

Lucas got into line behind a dozen other people. With luck he would just have time to get his food and eat it as he walked back to school.

"Is that you, Cabral? You punk." The voice was

harsh and challenging. Lucas steeled himself and turned around.

Two guys. One, short with a receding chin, a weedy red mustache, a reddish buzz cut, and dead blue eyes. The other, much larger, sullen, a shaved head, his muscular arms covered in crude tattoos. Both wore black jeans and steel-studded leather boots.

"Snake," Lucas said to the smaller of the two. "Did they finally let you go or did you escape?"

Snake smiled the fanged smile that gave him his name. "I hit eighteen, man. Birthday. The magic number."

"I didn't know you could count that high, Snake."

"Don't bust my balls, asswipe," Snake said. He jerked a thumb at the big guy. "Jones gets pissed when guys bust my balls."

Lucas thought of a smart remark but the truth was, while Snake by himself was a gutless little weasel, as part of a group he would be bolder. And Jones was big enough to be a group all by himself. "You know, Snake, I'd love to talk over old times, but you know, we're not supposed to be dealing with each other. It'd be a parole violation for you to be seen talking to a lowlife like me."

"Screw that. My parole officer's some old witch. I don't take any crap off her."

"You want something from me, Snake? Because if not, I think I'll bail. I didn't know they let people like you in here."

"Back to school like a good little boy, Cabral? Studying hard?" Snake stepped closer. "Or is it just the stuff, man. Is that it? You have some nice little piece warming you up at night, dude? Maybe a cheerleader or something? Yeah, I need to get me some of that. I been inside a long time, man. Maybe I could

49

just borrow yours for a few hours. What do you got, a blond? A redhead?" He nudged Jones and laughed. "She's a white girl at least, isn't she?"

Lucas's face froze. Suddenly he was out of the Burger King, far from Weymouth High, all the way back in a dark, loud, threatening place where the rules of normal behavior didn't apply. He moved closer to Snake, till his face was just inches from Snake's empty eyes.

"Don't get in my face, man. You'd better have more than this big dumb lump of crap backing you up before you get in my face."

To Lucas's surprise, Snake didn't back down. "I got all I need backing me up, Cabral. Dudes you don't even want to think about."

"More of your white-power morons?"

Snake blinked. "Like I said. We got some soldiers you don't want to think about messing with."

"Go crawl back under your rock," Lucas said in disgust. He pushed past Snake and headed for the exit. He threw the door open violently and sucked in the clear, cool outside air. He realized his hands were trembling, and he stuck them deep in his jeans pockets. He took several more deep breaths, trying to calm the quivering feeling in his stomach that was half fury, half fear.

He had known and dealt with guys like Snake in the Youth Authority. He'd almost gotten used to their simpleminded crudeness, the twisted, festering racism that had been nurtured in homes filled with hatred and alcoholic brutality. But here on the outside, back in the world, with all that now part of the past, it was a shock to see them again.

He wasn't really afraid, he told himself. Skinheads rarely took on people who could defend themselves.

And Lucas was wary enough to stay out of their way.

"Jesus," he muttered. "Six weeks ago I was listening to Snake whimpering in his sleep in the next bunk, and in three days I'm happy high school homecoming king." The contrast brought a wry smile to his lips.

He stretched to get the tension out of his neck and back, swung his arms to loosen the muscles that had tightened in preparation for sudden violence, and walked back to school. He would try to find Zoey, right away, even before sixth period when they would be in history together. If he could find her and hold her in his arms, she would drive the memories away.

"You're not eating that, are you?" Zoey looked at Nina in alarm. "That's tamale pie."

"I know it sucks, but I'm hungry," Nina said.

"It's beef, Nina. You don't eat dead cow or dead pig."

Nina shrugged. "It didn't make any sense, really. I mean, I ate dead fish and dead chicken. Besides, I'm allowed to change my mind." She took a tentative bite of the greasy mass.

"I was thinking about going *totally* veg," Aisha said accusingly. "You were my inspiration, Nina."

"I'm a work in progress, kids. I change, I grow, I gain new insights. Deal with it. Besides, I'm hungry."

Zoey looked over her shoulder. Claire was still coming through the lunch line. She might or might not decide to sit with them. Claire could just as easily decide to go off and sit alone. "Work in progress," she muttered, giving Nina a skeptical look. "So I hear, from third parties." She glanced meaningfully over her shoulder in the direction of Claire.

Nina looked mystified. Then her expression

cleared. "Oh. I was going to tell you; it's not some big secret or anything."

"You told your sister *before* you told me? Has there been some sudden outbreak of sisterly devotion at the Geiger household? *I'm* your first stop for new and fascinating gossip. Then *I* tell Aisha. That's the normal order of the universe."

Aisha nodded agreement. "We feel betrayed."

Nina sighed loudly. "Look, it's kind of embarrassing, okay? I didn't want you two going *aww, isn't it sweet, little Nina has a crush on Benjamin*."

Zoey smiled at Aisha. "It is sweet, though."

"Aww, look, she's blushing," Aisha said, pointing at Nina.

"Our little Nina is in love. You know, if things work out, she could someday be my sister-in-law."

"You'd be the aunt to her children."

"We'd have little family get-togethers and Nina and I would make fried chicken and coleslaw while the kids played out in the backyard and Lucas and Benjamin drank beer and belched."

Nina drummed her fingers on the table. "Are you two done?"

"All I can say is, watch out," Aisha advised. "Guys are basically pigs. Speaking of which. See that guy over there? The tall one? Do you think he'd like to take me to homecoming? I think he's better-looking than Christopher."

Claire had come up behind them. "Just because Christopher is a pig doesn't mean all guys are," she said. "And that guy you're looking at is a sophomore. He's just tall." She set down her tray and took the remaining seat.

"She's right, Eesh," Nina said. "You have to take a much broader sampling before you can say that all guys are pigs. Which is the only reason Claire keeps burning through guys at a rate of one every couple of months. Or, more recently, one in about a week.''

Claire sent Nina a tolerantly poisonous look. ''You know, it's really not fair, your taking cheap shots at me when you know that I can't fight back.''

''So fight back.''

''You're still in your official 'victim' status,'' Claire said. ''I'm trying to be a supportive sister and all, but you make it so difficult.''

Nina laughed. ''You don't have to treat me like I'm fragile. It's the opposite. I mean, what happened, happened a long time ago. Now that it's out in the open I feel *less* pathetic, not more. I'm now ruining *his* life, like he tried to ruin mine, so, to be honest with you, I feel pretty good. Better than I have since then.''

''Yeah, but I still can't pick on you for having had no love life,'' Claire said, shaking her head.

''We could pick on Aisha for always talking about how *she* was too smart to get caught up in some big romantic thing,'' Nina suggested.

''Go ahead, you're right,'' Aisha said, agreeing readily. ''I didn't listen to my own advice, and I ended up falling for some guy who's a weasel. Go ahead, give me your best shot. I deserve it.''

''It's no fun if you're asking for it,'' Nina grumbled.

''I have to admit one thing, though,'' Claire said. ''You handled it really well, Aisha. No weeping or wailing. Boom, it's over, get on with life. There's been like this epidemic of relationships breaking up lately,'' she observed. ''Zoey and Jake. Me and Benjamin. But Aisha's the cool one.''

Aisha smiled a little lopsidedly. ''It was never any big thing.''

"It must have been something fairly major. I mean, you were always above the fray, very cool about guys, and then suddenly you were hanging out with Christopher every time you got the chance."

"We barely ever saw you," Nina added, grimacing around her tamale pie.

"Talking about him. Engaging in public displays of making out and all. Jeez," Claire said, "that time I ran into you two out behind the gym after school, it was one of those scenes that should have been labeled 'young love,' or at least 'young passion.' You looked about ready to start a family." She paused to stare at Nina. "You're eating tamale pie?"

Aisha's face had fallen. She stared down at her tray.

"Let's talk about something else," Zoey said, pointedly giving Claire a look.

Claire looked at Aisha, then winced and sent Zoey a confused *how was I supposed to know* look.

"I've decided to eat dead stuff again," Nina said, trying to start the conversation in a new direction.

"I have to—" Aisha stood up and pointed vaguely in the direction of the door. "Some studying."

"Okay," Zoey said gently. "We'll see you later, Eesh."

Aisha fumbled picking up her books, and a tear dropped onto the table. Then she raced toward the exit.

Claire sat back and rolled her eyes. "Great. Maybe I should go after her."

"And display some more of that sensitivity you're famous for?" Nina asked.

"It's not Claire's fault," Zoey said. "You know Aisha. She always has to be so in control of everything. She keeps everything inside. She can't blame us for believing she really *is* in control."

Jake McRoyan stared blankly at the Xeroxed sheet on the desk in front of him. He had already written his name at the top, but at the moment that was the only thing he recognized on the page.

Since when did Ms. Rafanelli throw a surprise quiz at them on a Tuesday? She did quizzes on Thursday, not Tuesday.

He had actually made a brief effort to scan the assigned reading over the weekend. He'd looked at a few chapters, and it hadn't looked all that bad, as books went. The title involved bells for some reason, but it had been a war story. He'd rented a video of the movie that had been made from the book, but when he'd started to watch it with Lars Ehrlich, they'd decided to drink a few beers and take regular Nintendo 64 breaks, and with one thing or another they hadn't seen much of the movie, either.

1. *For Whom the Bell Tolls* **is the story of an American volunteer who fights in which war?**
   - ○ a. **The American Civil War**
   - ○ b. **The War of 1812.**
   - ○ c. **The Spanish Civil War**
   - ○ d. **The War of the Roses**

Well, forget *d*. Who would have a war and call it "The War of the Roses"? But it could be any of the first three choices.

"*C.*"

The whisper was barely audible, but it was real all the same. Claire, who sat behind him. Claire, who of course had read the book. She was as bad as Zoey when it came to homework. He'd hooked up with two little do-bees when it came to homework.

"Number one is *c*," Claire said.

The back of Jake's neck burned. Was he that obvious? Could she tell just by looking at the back of his head that he was clueless?

It made him furious. Just a few days earlier, Claire had rescued him with some homework he'd fallen behind on. Like he was some pity case all of a sudden.

Of course, in American lit. he was. He was holding on to a bare *C* −, and if it dropped to a *D*, he would be automatically suspended from the football team until he brought the grade back up.

His pencil hovered over the test. This was pathetic; it was just a little multiple-choice quiz to make sure people had read the book. It wasn't exactly a major essay test. Yet he'd been about to answer *a* when Claire had spoken. He'd have been wrong, because Claire definitely wasn't.

She was using this to get back on his good side. Like she'd tried to use the fact that she got him sobered up in time to make the last game.

His pencil still hovered.

He clenched his free hand into an angry fist. Damn Claire, anyway.

"Number two is *d*," the whispered voice said.

Ms. Rafanelli looked up, a puzzled expression on her face. She scanned the room for a moment, then went back to reading her book.

He could either write down the answers Claire was giving him and keep, maybe even slightly improve his low *C*, or he could ignore her, take the *D*, and be suspended for the homecoming game. He was furious at her. She was putting him in a terrible position. He couldn't keep taking her help and then go on treating her the way he had. It was sick. It was like she was seducing him, only with her . . . her niceness.

Claire. Nice. Right.

"Three is *a*."

This time Ms. Rafanelli looked up sharply and her focus was narrower. She knew the section of the room where the subtle sound of cheating was coming from. She probably guessed it was him. Could probably tell from the way he just sat there, with his pencil frozen in midair, looking pissed off, that it was him.

Do it or don't do it, he ordered himself.

He would never accept her help again. That was his decision. After this, never again.

He wrote down the answers in quick succession.

4. Hemingway is considered—

Jake felt a sharp fingernail pressing into his back. He controlled his reaction, keeping his eyes down on his paper. Claire drew her fingernail over the flesh of his back, drawing a distinct *4*, followed by the letter *c*. It sent chills through him. He could feel his resolve draining away with each contact.

The next six questions went the same way. He would have an *A* on the quiz. It might be enough to raise him to a solid *C* in the class. He would stay on the team.

The bell rang and he got up, feeling stiff and exhausted, as if he had just gone through some terrible ordeal. He didn't want to look at her, to let her see in his eyes the power her simple touch had over him.

He left quickly and headed directly down the hall toward his next class. But she was at his side.

"Don't bother to say thanks or anything," Claire said.

"I didn't ask for your help," Jake muttered without looking at her.

"Yeah, but you'll get a ninety on the test."

"Ninety?" He stopped and stared. A mistake. He would never be able to stay angry at her when he was looking into her eyes.

She smiled her half smile. "Rafanelli would never buy you getting a perfect score, Jake. I gave you the wrong answer for question five. And I gave myself the wrong answer for question seven. That way it won't look like we cheated."

He shook his head in frank admiration. "Sometimes you're just scary, Claire."

"Thanks, I guess."

"What do you want from me?"

She seemed to consider the question for a moment. "I want you to love me, Jake. I want you to forgive me for what happened two years ago."

Jake met her level, unwavering gaze. Love her? Of course he loved her. The mere touch of her finger on his back had electrified him, setting off reactions he couldn't control, desires he couldn't turn off. If he could only stop loving her, his life might go back to normal. He might not see her face every night in the dark as he lay in bed. The memory of her might not war constantly in his brain with the memory of his brother.

Love me, Jake. Forgive me, Jake.

"One out of two isn't bad," he said sadly.

Five

Mrs. Gray gave the shallow pan a shake. "Are you ready, Aisha?"

"Ready." Aisha had four prechilled bowls of vanilla ice cream waiting in the freezer.

"Okay, bring them out. Kalif, turn off the lights."

The lights went out. Mrs. Gray poured a long stream of kirschwasser into the pan, then tilted the pan so the bubbling liquid nearly spilled into the fire of the stove. In an instant the pan went up in a brilliant flash, then settled down into gentler blue tongues of flame.

From the table Mr. Gray applauded. Mrs. Gray quickly spooned the cherries jubilee over the ice cream and Aisha just as quickly shuttled the bowls to the table.

"Excellent," Aisha said enthusiastically, spooning up a bite. "You could open a restaurant and give Zoey's parents some competition."

Her mother smiled at the compliment. "Thanks, but a bed-and-breakfast is work enough. I don't know how the Passmores do it, breakfast, lunch, and dinner every day. They must live in that restaurant."

"Zoey says they just about do," Aisha said.

They were eating in the breakfast room, a part of

the house reserved for guests when the tourist season brought people to the bed-and-breakfast. As fall advanced, though, there were fewer guests and the Gray family gradually reclaimed more of the huge building.

"Saw a red phalarope today," Aisha's father said.

Kalif rolled his eyes. Aisha smiled. Her little brother was at the age where their father just embarrassed him.

"*Phalaropus fulicarius* in Latin," Mr. Gray said.

"What did it look like?" Aisha asked, mostly out of politeness, but at least partly from real interest.

"Well, it was in its winter plumage, gray and white. Has a call like *Peek! Peek!*"

Kalif looked alarmed, and Aisha smothered a smile. The spectacle of her bookish, conservative father suddenly exploding in loud bird noises, something he did regularly, was so incongruous it was hard not to crack up. He was a librarian at the Weymouth main public library, a place where he fit in perfectly, unlike here in his own house with his younger, more energetic wife and his compulsively athletic son.

Aisha was closest to him in temperament. They were both intellectual, reserved, not very emotional people. And to her own surprise, Aisha actually had started noticing the birds that lived on or passed by the island.

"Coffee, honey?" Mrs. Gray asked her husband.

"Just half a cup."

"I want some, too," Aisha said.

Her mother gave her a look. "Since when do you drink coffee?"

"I have a lot of homework to do," Aisha said.

Her mother brought the coffee to the table and poured for Aisha and her father. "What homework do you have?"

"Calc, biology, French, you name it."

Kalif cracked his knuckles loudly. "Pressure getting to you? Huh? Huh? Going to crack? Going to lose it?"

"Is all *your* homework done, Kalif?"

"I knew I shouldn't have said anything."

"I was going to see if you wanted to go out to the mall tomorrow after school," Mrs. Gray said. "Tomorrow's Wednesday; the homecoming dance is on Saturday."

Aisha shrugged. "I don't need to go to the mall," she said nonchalantly.

"Don't you want to get something new to wear? The only things you have for dances are getting a little tight on you."

"What with you getting fat," Kalif interjected.

"Don't press the girl if she doesn't want to spend money on a dress," Mr. Gray said mildly.

"She can't go looking shabby, Alan," Mrs. Gray said.

"Actually, I don't think I'm going at all," Aisha said.

"Uh-oh, trouble in the land of lo-o-ove," Kalif said gleefully.

"You're not going to homecoming?"

Aisha shrugged. "Maybe, maybe not. It's no big deal."

"Are you having a problem with Christopher?" her mother inquired, trying her best not to sound like she was prying.

She *was* prying, and Aisha didn't appreciate it. "He's not even in school," she said evasively. "Homecoming is for students."

"Yep. Trouble," Kalif opined. "I'm not surprised. Christopher was always way too cool for you."

61

"Kalif, finish going through puberty first, then start worrying about other people's lives," Aisha said. "Look, I'm just not all that into dances and stuff, anyway. I go to school to learn, right? Isn't that the idea?"

"She has you there, Carol," Mr. Gray said.

His wife was undeterred. "Yes, you go to learn, but I thought you were going to this dance with Christopher, that's all. I just need to know whether you're going to want a new dress; that's my only interest in the matter. Kalif, clear the table. It's your turn with dishes."

"So what'd he do, dump you?" Kalif asked.

"No, not that it's any of your scrotelike business, but I dumped him. Actually."

"Big mistake. He was way cool."

"He was a jerk," Aisha said hotly. "And if I wanted to go to the stupid dance, I could easily find a date. Plenty of guys have asked me out."

"Yeah, right. *Human* guys?"

"Kalif, that's enough," Mr. Gray said quietly.

Aisha noticed her mother looking at her with an expression very close to pity.

"It's no big deal," Aisha practically yelled.

"As long as you're okay," her mother said in her concerned voice.

"Look. I caught him with some other girl, all right? So he's a toad, all right? So he's out of my life, all right? So forget about him. *I* have." She took a last sip of her coffee. "Now, *I* have homework to do. You can all sit around and discuss my private life if you want, but I'm busy."

She turned with perfect control and began walking away. Her mother caught up to her at her bedroom door.

62

"Mother," Aisha said patiently. She only called her mother *mother* when she was annoyed. "I don't need a little heart-to-heart talk, okay?"

Her mother held up her hands in a gesture of innocence. "Not me. I was just going to say if he was trying to pressure you into sleeping with him, you did the right thing, dumping him."

Aisha felt weary. "Of course he was pressuring me. Guys usually do, but I know how you feel about that and I know how I feel about that. It wasn't about sex. It was what I said—I walked in on him and this girl and then he lied to me about seventy-five times in less than five minutes."

"So you dumped him for being a two-timing liar?"

Aisha sighed. "Yes, Mother."

Her mother grabbed her and crushed her in a hug. "My girl," she said proudly. "Teach that boy a lesson."

"I thought you really liked Christopher."

"I do. Or I did. But if he's going to lie to you, then bye-bye."

"Bye-bye," Aisha repeated.

"There are other boys. Find someone else to go to the dance with."

"You mean so I can rub Christopher's nose in it."

"Of course. How do you think your father and I got together the first time? Your father was the guy I went out with just to get back at my old boyfriend."

"So, you been working on your romance novel lately?" Nina asked. She was lying on her back on the floor of Zoey's room, throwing a troll doll someone had given Zoey up in the air and trying to catch it. Unfortunately, Nina was no athlete and she kept banging the hard plastic doll against the sloped ceiling, making a loud noise and distracting Zoey from her homework.

"No. Not lately," Zoey muttered. She was sitting at the desk in her dormered window, trying to compose a story for her journalism class. It was supposed to be an account of a speech the president had given on tax reform. It had not been an exciting speech, and every time she tried to read the printed version of it, her mind wandered off. Writing a story about a speech you couldn't force yourself to actually read was a challenge.

Nina threw the troll into the air. It hit the slanted ceiling, took a bad bounce, and landed on Zoey's head.

"Nina!"

"Sorry."

"I have a stuffed bear you could throw. It's soft."

"So are you ever going to let me read any of your romance novel?"

Zoey shook her head definitely. "No. First of all, it's not a novel. It's just a first chapter rewritten about twenty times. Second of all, you would laugh."

"Maybe not."

Zoey put down her pencil and rubbed her forehead. "I can't even write *this* stupid story. I'm not exactly ready to start writing romance novels."

Nina sat up. "Maybe it's the subject matter. Maybe you have a good feel for romance and you aren't into politics."

"I don't know that I'm an expert on romance," Zoey said dryly. "Now, Claire would be an expert."

"Yeah, well, I'm a total amateur and I can't ask Claire," Nina said, her sentence trailing off into a low mutter.

Zoey looked at her. "What are you talking about, Nina?" Nina was seldom so indirect.

Her friend shrugged. "I was just saying I don't know very much about all that stuff. I mean, I've only ever kissed one guy—I mean, voluntarily—and then I practically gacked up a kidney."

"Oh. Are you worried about going out with Benjamin?"

"Worried? Not worried, really. Quivering in terror, sure. It's just that I'm not very experienced. I'm like a Muslim in a liquor store. I'm like a Republican trying to understand rap lyrics."

Zoey waited patiently. Nina followed what she called her three-part comic tautology rule—funny examples should come in threes.

"Hang on, I'm thinking," Nina said, wrinkling her brow. "Okay. I'm like a fashion model in a bookstore. Come on, that one's good."

"So, you're saying you feel lost, confused, intimidated?"

"Yes, yes, help me, please." She clasped her hands in supplication.

"What is it you want to know?" Zoey said, feeling a little uncomfortable. After all, Nina was going to be out with her brother.

"All the dating protocol. You know, do you hold hands? If you do hold hands, is it just like shaking-hands style, or interlocked fingers, and what if your hand gets sweaty, and how do you know when to stop?"

"Well, Nina, really it's kind of up to you. I mean, what do you feel comfortable doing?"

"I don't feel *comfortable* doing anything. Not to be gross, but when I like even think about kissing a guy or whatever . . . especially whatever . . . I get these flashes back to my uncle and all. It's not like I'm hallucinating or going schizo; it's just I start thinking about it and it makes me sick.''

"It's not gross, Nina, it's just kind of sad," Zoey said gently. "I mean, the whole dating thing is weird enough without adding extra levels of weirdness.''

"I thought maybe if I could get used to the idea ahead of time, I could deal with it when it happens. Like when I have to go to my gynecologist, I spend a week ahead of time going, 'It's okay, she's a doctor, she's not going to hurt you, she's just a nice old lady with no sense of humor,' and so on. I even write out little scenarios. You know, like I'll write that I'll go in, lose it, and end up running out into the street wearing one of those paper dresses they give you. Then when I'm there, it's just unpleasant, as opposed to terrifying.''

"Well, no one exactly enjoys being in those stirrups," Zoey admitted. "Believe me, whatever happens between you and Benjamin, it won't be *that* unpleasant." She shook her head. "I can't believe I'm talking about this.''

"So, show me how to hold hands the right way," Nina said.

Zoey scooted down to the floor beside Nina, feeling thoroughly foolish. She sat facing the same direction as Nina, side by side. "Okay, say you're at a movie.''

"You're at a movie.''

"Are you going to be making jokes all the way through this?" Zoey asked.

"So, we're at a movie.''

"Put your hand like it's on the armrest.''

"Why?''

"Because if you want him to hold your hand, you don't want to have your hand in your lap, right?''

66

Zoey explained. "I mean, make it easy for the guy. You want him to have to rummage around in your lap looking for your hand?"

"No, then I would definitely hurl," Nina said. "We'd be talking supersonic popcorn." She held her hand up on an imaginary armrest.

Zoey ran her fingers through her hair, fiddled with the neck of her shirt, wiped her hands on her shorts.

"What are you doing?"

"I'm being the guy," Zoey said. "They usually take a while to get their nerve up." She let her hand creep along the imaginary armrest, until her elbow was resting and the side of her hand was touching the side of Nina's hand.

"Is that it?" Nina demanded.

"This is just phase one. He wants to see if you'll yank your hand away."

"Will I?" Nina asked anxiously. "I mean, should I?"

"No, Nina. You keep up the contact. Then, after a while he gets up his nerve to make the big jump." She slid her hand over Nina's.

"What do I do?"

"I would do this." Zoey turned her hand palm up and interlaced her fingers with Nina's.

"Okay."

"That's it."

"Doesn't seem like much," Nina said, sounding a little disappointed.

"It will seem like a lot more when it's a guy," Zoey reassured her.

"Yeah, that's what worries me. But I guess I can handle this. As long as I don't have to kiss or any-thing."

"Good, because I'm not about to teach you that," Zoey said.

"Maybe if it was just a little kiss-on-the-cheek kind of thing. Like a Hollywood air kiss."

Zoey smiled at Nina, still holding her hand. "Don't worry so much. It's Benjamin. Which, by the way, has advantages. You don't have to worry about long, lingering looks deep into each other's eyes. Also, you can go the whole night with a piece of spinach stuck in your teeth without him ever noticing."

"Yeah."

"It will all be fine. You won't panic and you won't hurl."

"It's not like I don't feel all those romantic kind of things," Nina said in a dreamy, reflective voice. "I do. I mean, you know, all those things you feel about guys."

"Yes, I know those things," Zoey said dryly. She thought back to the first time she had kissed Lucas. And the most recent time. She sighed.

"Mmm. Um, Zoey?"

"Yes?"

"We're still holding hands. I mean, I like you and all, but . . ."

BENJAMIN

Good TV shows for a blind person
are, first of all, talk shows. Obviously.
They're mostly ~~conservation~~ conversation and not much reliance on visuals.
Also, comedy of any kind except jug-
gling and Carrot Top. Although, from
what people tell me, Carrot Top's not
very funny even if you can see. MTV is
great, although I don't see the video
part. But again, people tell me maybe
that's a good thing.

Nature shows, documentaries, anything on the Discovery Channel, you can
forget. Ten minutes at a time of the
sounds of wind whistling across the sa-
vannah and then the narrator comes on
and says, "The lion pride has moved off
through the trees," followed by another
ten minutes of wind sounds.

By the same token, there are people
who are good for blind people and others ~~hwo~~ who aren't. What you want
are people who talk, and when they
talk they have something to say. Gen-
erally, girls are better at expressing
themselves in words, and so I've
tended to have more female friends
than male.

Convenient, huh?

Take Lucas. I like him, but the guy doesn't have a lot to say most of the time. Jake is even worse. He could be in the room for an hour and I wouldn't know it unless he farted or cleared his throat or something. Whereas when my sister's around, she usually has something to say and she says it well. She'll make a good writer someday ~~because~~ because when you ask her to describe something, she can make it come alive.

Her friend Aisha is the exception to the rule about girls. Very internalized, which may be great for her, but makes her almost invisible to me at times.

Now, Nina, as my father would say in one of his flashback-to-the-seventies moments, is a trip. Listening to Nina is almost like hearing a performance of some sort. She has fun with words. Her own, mine, anyone's. It's one of the reasons I love to have her read to me. She doesn't just read; she interprets. She sort of <u>acts</u> the book, although I don't think she's even aware of it.

Then there's Claire. Not a very talkative person, really. She only makes small talk to be polite. Claire keeps her secrets, and the biggest secret she keeps is her real self. Why I was ever interested in her to begin with, I ~~coulnd't~~ couldn't say. Maybe <u>because</u> she was so withdrawn. I couldn't look into her eyes, or read her expression, or interpret her body language. I could only listen to her words and from those few clues try to understand a girl who did not want to be understood.

Later, though, there was touch. And not even Claire can conceal the meaning of a racing pulse, a tremor, a soft yielding, a sudden sharp intake of breath.

Six

On Tuesday night Christopher left Passmores', the restaurant owned by Zoey's parents, at eleven twenty-five, after sending out the last late order, changing the fat in the deep fryers, stoning the grill, finishing up the dishwashing, prepping pancake batter for the morning shift, sweeping and mopping the kitchen, mopping out the walk-in, turning off the lights, and locking the doors.

He rode his bike to his apartment, watched the Top Ten list on *Letterman*, and fell asleep just before midnight, the remote control still in his hand.

Three hours later, his alarm went off. He made a cup of coffee, spooned up a bowl of Grape-Nuts, showered, dressed, and was on his bike, heading toward the ferry landing by three twenty-five A.M.

The bundled newspapers from Weymouth, Portland, and Boston, and of course the *Wall Street Journal*, lay wrapped in heavy plastic on the dock. It was still pitch-black out, and he was the only person awake in North Harbor or any other part of Chatham Island. It was cold enough to make his breath steam, and his hands had grown numb during the brief bike trip. Tomorrow he would have to remember gloves. And when it got really cold in the hard winter months,

72

well, he had no idea what he'd do. He'd probably have to buy an island car.

He divided the newspapers. The heavy *Boston Globe*s in his backpack, the other papers apportioned in the two saddlebags.

He rode the easy parts of the route first, following level, smoothly paved Lighthouse Road, throwing a rubber-banded *Portland Press-Herald* here, a *Weymouth Times* there. Claire and Nina's house, dark and silent, got all four. Mr. Geiger liked plenty to read on his morning ferry ride to work.

Gradually the load grew lighter, and Christopher took on the teeth-rattling cobblestoned streets and the steep slopes that circled the base of the hill.

The two-thirds point in his route was Aisha's home. It was up a backbreaking hill, winding to the top of the ridge. He always paused and rested after reaching it. He deposited their two newspapers and rested his bike against the fence.

He had never been in Aisha's room, but he thought he knew where it was from her casual descriptions. It was around the right and toward the back.

Feeling a little foolish, he walked through the garden across frosted pine needles that crunched like cornflakes and located her two windows. He was disappointed to see that there was no light from inside. He would have loved to have looked at her. He had his fantasy that someday she would start setting her alarm for this time of morning. She would welcome him through her window and into her warm bed. Then he would go on with his route and she would go back to sleep, both of them happy and satisfied.

"Not likely," he muttered under his breath.

He headed back to his bike and finished the outer reaches of his route, the long easy coast back down the hill, the big, extended circle going down along the eastern shore around Big Bite Pond, then back to his apartment on the western shore.

By five he was done. He parked his bike and fell into his bed facedown.

He slept until seven, got up, biked to an empty house on Coast Road where he was installing storm shutters, worked till nine, rode to the ferry landing, and caught the water taxi over to Weymouth. The water taxi was free to him for the season, in exchange for work he had done during the summer, scraping and repainting the boat. On the trip over he caught fifteen minutes' sleep hunched over on the bench.

He arrived at Weymouth High just before ten and immediately began organizing the sports equipment room, cleaning balls, replacing torn basketball nets, and running equipment out to the field for the boys' and girls' gym classes.

On good days, this was his easy job, affording him ten minutes of sleep here, fifteen minutes there, crashed out on a soft pile of gym mats between classes.

He was scheduled to cook that night, and at the end of the workday at school he would catch the next ferry or water taxi and start setting up the kitchen for his shift.

He usually had one or two evenings a week free, but this wasn't one of them.

Not counting the work he did around the apartment building in exchange for reduced rent, he averaged seventy-five hours a week of work, earning a total take-home income of about four hundred dollars a week. So far he had saved nearly three thousand dollars. By the end of next summer he would have the tuition, room, and board for his first year of college.

Then, with hard studying and a clean academic record, he could go for student loans and grants and even a scholarship. He would have to overcome a weak high school record to make it into a good college. Without anyone's help. Without relying on anyone but himself.

It was a hard life, and he was entitled, he felt, to a little comfort where and when he could get it. Something Aisha just didn't seem to understand. He wasn't trying to pressure Aisha into it because the truth was, someday, way down the road, he could see the two of them together. Married, maybe. It was possible.

But what was not possible was that monogamy would start now. Especially a celibate monogamy. The pursuit of his goals already denied him any kind of life, and that was all the self-denial he could take.

Right now, living this life, he felt he needed more than promises of someday, someday . . .

Nina finished telling her story and looked as boldly as she could manage at the psychiatrist. Dr. Kendall nodded several times and looked at her thoughtfully.

"And what is being done now about your uncle?"

Nina shrugged. "My dad has his lawyer talking to a lawyer in Minnesota about talking to the prosecutor there. Legal stuff. My dad said we might not know anything definite for quite a while."

"And how does that make you feel?"

"Claire warned me you liked to ask that question."

Dr. Kendall smiled. "How is Claire? She's stopped coming."

"Well, you know Claire. Actually, you *do* know Claire. Nothing gets my sister down for long. She always copes. But then, who am I to tell you this, right?"

"Actually, that's pretty close to my own feelings about Claire. Considering the death of your mother and the events of the accident and all that followed . . ." She raised her eyebrows philosophically. "She's a very adaptive person."

"How about me? Will I be needing shock therapy? I hear it's kind of a fun high."

Dr. Kendall looked alarmed, then laughed uneasily. "No, I don't think electroconvulsive therapy is necessary, Nina. I think maybe just weekly sessions for a while."

"The truth is, I feel fine. I mean, actually, I feel better than I usually do. If anything, I've been kind of up, you know? People keep coming over to me all droopy-eyed, asking me how I'm doing, and half the time I forget what they're talking about. Then it's like, oh yeah, *that*. I was hoping to be able to tell them all I was getting shock therapy, then kind of give a little spaz." She demonstrated, jerking her neck to one side and twisting her mouth. "I guess I could still *tell* them I was getting the juice."

"Why would you want to do that?"

Nina smiled. "My *other* therapist is an expert in getting people to drop the pity routine. He's blind."

"The same boy your sister was seeing?"

"Benjamin, right. There aren't a lot of blind guys around in school, just him. When he went blind, he started making a thing of it, you know? Like in his room he has posters up on the walls, only half of them are upside down. When people come over for the first time, he'll talk about how proud he is of this great art print and it will be like a map of Poland or something. Some people are very slow to get the joke, or else they'll play along because they think he'll have a breakdown if they tell him the truth."

76

"I see. He makes a joke out of his blindness."

"Yeah, but it's *his* joke. No one can make fun of him because whatever they're going to say, Benjamin's already said it better and funnier." Nina smiled and for a moment almost forgot where she was. "He's basically the coolest human being I know. His parents pay me to read to him sometimes and he's just so . . . I don't know. He's just very, very cool."

"Is there some romantic interest here?"

Nina snapped back to reality. The word *romantic* surprised her. "We're going out on a date this weekend," she admitted.

"Do you feel comfortable going out on a date so soon after what's happened?"

Nina nodded. "With Benjamin, sure. It's not like he's going to try and drag me off to a Motel 6."

"He's someone you can trust."

"Yes," Nina said softly. "I trust Benjamin."

"And your sister?"

"No, I don't trust her at all," Nina said quickly, although what the shrink meant was obvious.

"I meant to say is this a comfortable thing between you and Claire, that you're going out with her former boyfriend?"

"He told me he's still kind of in love with her," Nina admitted. "Of course, so are half the guys in school."

Dr. Kendall glanced at her watch. "Our hour is about up, Nina. I think we've had a very productive first session. I want to leave you with one thing to bear in mind—you may be a little vulnerable right now. Incest and molestation are not minor events. You won't be able to just put them behind you as easily as you'd like."

Nina nodded.

"In the meantime, go slow with this boy Benjamin, okay? Give yourself some time to adjust to normal relationships with members of the opposite sex."

"I've given myself sixteen years, so far," Nina said.

"Mmm. Don't be in a hurry. But have fun."

"Okay." Nina stood up and stretched up on her toes. She rarely sat still for this long. "So, before I go, just tell me one thing. When they do the shock treatment, do they stick something in your mouth so you don't bite your tongue off?"

Seven

Zoey's mother had spent the afternoon at the oral surgeon having a molar removed. She was high on codeine and not in a condition to work. Mrs. Toombs, who worked as a waitress, was in Lewiston visiting her son and her daughter-in-law. Christopher was cooking, which left Zoey to handle the restaurant for the night, waiting on any tables and tending the bar.

Her father had asked whether she could handle it so he could stay home with her mother. Zoey had said yes, she could handle it as long as she got bartender pay, which was higher than waiter pay.

To Zoey's annoyance, there was a strong early dinner rush that had her running like a rat in a maze from dining room to bar to kitchen and around again. But by eight it had calmed down considerably. In fact, there was just one table occupied and some regulars at the bar who wouldn't mind pouring their own drinks if Zoey wasn't handy.

She pushed open the kitchen door, tore the top slip off the ticket, and slapped it down on the stainless steel counter that separated her from Christopher.

"Ordering," she said.

"You got much more out there, Zo?" Christopher asked, reading the ticket. His hands began to move automatically, pulling a metal plate of fish from the reach-in, bending over to get a steak and tossing it casually onto the grill, checking to see if he had sufficient baked potatoes. "I'll give 'em two small lobsters, okay? All I have left are small."

"They won't mind that," Zoey said wearily. "This will probably be the last table unless we're just cursed. Thanks for coming out there and busing those tables. You didn't have to do that, although if you hadn't, I'd be dead by now."

"No prob."

Zoey slid up onto the counter, grateful for the opportunity to take the load off her feet for a moment. She picked at a run in her panty hose. "It's times like this I wished I smoked or drank or something. Some little ritual so I would know I was taking a break."

Christopher checked the steak, glanced at the fish, and began methodically garnishing the plates. "So, Zoey. What has Aisha told you?" He kept his eyes down on his work, trying to look uninterested.

Zoey shrugged. "She mentioned you were more or less broken up."

"More or less? She said more or less?"

"Actually, closer to *more*. But I don't think I should be talking to you about this. Aisha's my friend."

"And I'm not?" He smiled winningly.

"You're my friend, too," Zoey said quickly, wishing she could just avoid this. She was sure to end up pissing off either Christopher or Aisha. Or maybe both of them. "It's a girl thing."

"Yeah, well, you know, I'm crazy about Aisha. I wish we could work something out." He was back to concentrating on his work. He moved away to turn the steak and poke at the lobsters. "I mean, I don't

80

want it to end like this. It wasn't my idea.''

Zoey started to say something, then stopped herself. Then she said it anyway. ''Wasn't there some other girl?''

He shrugged. ''That didn't mean anything.''

''Then why was she in your room if she didn't mean anything?'' Zoey demanded in exasperation.

He shrugged again. ''She was hot-looking.''

''Well, then, I guess you were totally helpless. What could you do if she was hot-looking?''

''I never told Aisha it was a strict one-on-one thing,'' Christopher pointed out.

''You never told her it wasn't, either. You should have figured out she'd be hurt.''

Christopher winced. ''That's just about exactly what your boyfriend told me.''

''Lucas?''

''Do you have another?''

''Lucas knew you were seeing this other girl?'' Zoey asked.

Christopher made a face. ''Oh. Suddenly I have the feeling I should have kept my mouth shut.''

Lucas knew? And he hadn't told *her*? He'd let Aisha walk into that scene and be humiliated? In a flash she remembered the way Lucas had sort of done a double take the day Aisha had shown up on the verge of tears and mentioned another girl. Part of her was relieved. She'd wondered if Lucas was reacting out of some personal guilt.

''It was a guy thing,'' Christopher explained helpfully.

''I'd better go check on the dining room,'' Zoey said, hopping down from the counter.

''Great, now Lucas will be pissed at me, too.''

''I won't tell him you told me,'' Zoey promised.

81

"Look, Zo, what I really wanted to ask was whether maybe you could talk to Aisha. You know, see if there's any way we can maybe get past this." He shook his head ruefully. "I miss her. I'd appreciate it if you'd tell her that for me. That's all, just tell her I miss her."

"Okay. Scenario one," Nina said. She was in her room, lying on her bed, feet propped on the wall, staring up at a poster of the Red Hot Chili Peppers. Her stereo was playing a Smashing Pumpkins CD, just loudly enough that no one would be able to hear her talking to herself.

"It's Saturday night, we're supposed to meet at the ferry, he decides not to show up. There I am, standing around with Zoey and Lucas and Jake and Eesh. And Claire, who laughs and says, 'What did you expect? Like Benjamin would want to go out with you?' "

Nina considered the scenario for a moment. Not so bad, really. A little humiliating, but she could get over it and the real pressure would be off.

"Okay. Something better. Scenario two. Um, we go to the dance, we walk in together, the music stops, everyone stops talking and stares at us. Then they start laughing."

The humiliation level would be much higher because it would involve a lot more people. And they would all be thinking *Oh, look, Nina's pretending to like guys. Isn't Benjamin sweet to play along with her?*

Still, as unpleasant as that was, it wasn't getting to what really scared her.

"Scenario three. And you'll like this one, Flea," she told the poster. "We go to the dance, and then we have to slow dance, he puts his arms around me, and boom, flashback time. All the feelings start and I panic. I run screaming from the room while waves of laughter mixed with pity pursue me. Yeah, that's more like it.''

Unfortunately, it wasn't possible to completely dismiss the scenario. In the recesses of her mind, a male's touch, any male, meant only one thing. She'd been eleven years old when her uncle had begun two months of almost nightly abuse. Old enough to know what was going on. Old enough to form detailed, precise, lurid memories full of his touch and the sound of his voice. Memories of shame and self-loathing, of wishing she were dead, of wishing she were horribly disfigured so that he wouldn't want her anymore. Memories that haunted her sleep and came boiling up to the surface whenever she felt sexually threatened. And a threat could be something very innocuous. At those times she felt like some timid wild creature like a deer, easily startled, ready to run from anything in blind panic.

Once a guy, a perfectly nice guy, had tried to kiss her, and she'd nearly thrown up. It was one of the events that had people believing she was gay. Or else wondering if she really was as crazy as she sometimes pretended to be.

"Scenario four. The dreaded kiss. We've danced, we've joked around, we've done whatever, and now he wants to kiss me. Or else he really doesn't want to but he figures it's the polite thing to do after the date. He leans close, and it's suddenly like I'm back *there*.''

The image alone was deeply disturbing. It was a strange, churning mix of conflicting feelings. Part of her wanted Benjamin to kiss her. Really, really wanted. But another part of her grew sick at the thought of a man's mouth pressed against her own. Of a man's hands on her body.

"Stop it!" Nina cried. She rolled over and off the bed. She went to the CD player and turned it off. Then she sat down in a chair and leaned forward, keeping her head between her knees to fight off the wave of nausea.

This was how she would behave on Saturday night. She could feel it. She could see the moment as if it had already happened. It would be the end. Not even Benjamin was that tolerant or patient. No guy ever would be.

Zoey was out of the restaurant by ten, leaving it to Christopher to close up for the night. She left carrying the zippered plastic deposit bag with the night's receipts. There was a tiny bank branch on the circle, installed there by Mr. Geiger as a convenience for his fellow Chatham Islanders.

The cobblestoned streets were deserted and dark, even at this relatively early hour. The only nightlife the island had was in the two restaurants, her parents' and Topsider's, which was just closing as she passed by.

She trudged on bruised feet up Exchange, feeling the sense of safety that was one of the best things about living on an island. Over in Weymouth there might be the occasional holdup or rape, but even the densest criminals knew better than to try to operate on an island with three hundred residents and the only escape route by ferry.

She reached the garish, fluorescent automatic teller machine and the drop box. She fished out the key and slid the bank bag inside. Then she headed toward home, circumnavigating the circle.

Something caught her eye, a movement from the grassy center of the circle. She peered closely and, even in the mix of streetlight and starlight, could see that it was Jake.

"Hey, Zoey," he said, raising a languid hand. He sat slumped back on a bench.

Zoey smiled awkwardly. Since their breakup, she and Jake had steered clear of each other—as much as you could when you both had to take the same ferry twice a day and share three classes.

She wasn't sure if he was just being polite or if he expected her to stop by. She decided the polite and decent thing to do was cross into the circle.

"You're out late," he said. "Work?"

"Yeah. My mom had some work done on her teeth."

"Uh huh. How's biz?"

She shrugged. It was odd, talking to him without other people around. Once they would have been sitting here together, making out and planning what they were going to do the next day or the rest of their lives. "I did okay on tips." She jangled the money stuffed in her pockets, a wad of quarters and singles and a few fives. "What are you doing out here?"

"Not a damned thing," he said flatly.

"Taking it easy, huh?"

"Yep. I guess that's it. I guess I'm taking it easy."

Again she was at a loss for something to say. Jake seemed like he'd been drinking, or else he was just very tired. His eyes were sad, but the rest of his face was frozen in a blank expression. He was breathing heavily, as though the air was thick.

"That was a pretty strange scene last weekend, huh? You know, with Nina and all," Zoey finally said.

He dropped his head forward and jerked it up and down twice in a nod. "Yeah. Yeah."

"Well. I guess I'd better head on home." She forced a tinny laugh. "See if my mom's OD'd on painkillers yet. She hates going to the dentist."

Jake said nothing, just stared down at the sparse grass.

"Anyway. Bye." She turned and took two steps before stopping and turning back. "Jake, are you okay?"

"Okay?" He lifted his head. "I'm always okay, Zoey."

"It's just that you seem depressed."

"Now, why would I be depressed?" There was the telltale edge of sarcasm in his voice, but even that was tired.

Zoey felt a flash of anger. It wasn't like Jake to wallow in self-pity. Look how Nina was dealing with her problems. She wasn't turning into a drunk and feeling sorry for herself. Or Lucas. And his life wasn't exactly a day at Disney World.

But in hot pursuit of her anger came guilt. She had been the one to dump Jake. Then, in almost no time at all, his relationship with Claire had fallen apart. He'd been on a real roller coaster emotionally, and at least a part of that was her fault.

"Look, Jake, I'm sorry things worked out the way they did for you. You're the nicest guy on earth, and you deserve better."

"No. Wade was the nicest guy on earth," he said. Now the slur in his speech was obvious.

He was drunk. Again. If he kept this up, he was going to develop a problem. Maybe he already had. "Look, I know he was your brother and all, but he wasn't very nice, really. Wade was a bully. I used to hate the way he treated you."

Jake stared at her like she was talking gibberish. "He was tough, see? He was—" He hesitated, at a loss for words. "He always said I was a wuss."

"He was wrong, Jake. He was just giving you a hard time."

"He was *right*." Jake emphasized the point by stabbing his finger at her.

"Jake, have you been drinking? You never used to drink."

"I've discovered I have a talent for it," he said, grinning.

Again Zoey realized how out of place she felt. It was amazing that such a wall could grow up so quickly between two people who had been close. "Jake, if you ever want to just talk . . . I'm still your friend."

"Thanks, Zo," he said softly.

"You should head home. School tomorrow and all." She clasped her arms tightly around herself to show that she was cold. "Besides, you don't want to get pneumonia."

"I'll do that, Zoey," he said. "I'll head home in just a little while."

"Good night," she said.

He didn't answer.

Eight

Midnight

Zoey woke from a fitful sleep. The Boston Bruins shirt she slept in had become twisted. She flopped around to straighten it out and by the time she was done, she was wide awake. She got up and went over to the dormered window where she had a built-in desk. On one wall of the dormer were yellow Post-it notes she used to tack up great quotes, things to think about on nights when she couldn't sleep.

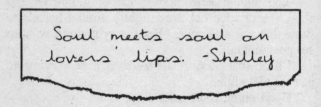

Soul meets soul on lovers' lips. -Shelley

She'd found the quote and posted it, thinking of Lucas. But now she found she was remembering Jake, so sad sitting in the dark circle. She had kissed Jake many more times over the years than she had Lucas. She had never felt for Jake the sort of overwhelming feeling she had for Lucas, but she had loved him nevertheless. And it seemed wrong to now just dismiss him from her mind when he seemed to need help.

Jake had always had an overdeveloped sense of duty. He felt bound by some loyalty to his dead brother. And yet he had always been an emotional guy. When he fell in love, he fell hard. And now he was caught between being loyal to his brother and hopelessly in love with Claire, the girl he blamed for his brother's death.

But how could Zoey help him? How could anyone, really, when the battle was all between Jake and Jake?

12:45 A.M.

Nina got up to pee, cursing the Pepsi she'd drunk before going to bed. The floor was cold under her bare feet, and after getting back to her room, she hopped back into bed and tucked the blankets around her toes.

Then she remembered she'd been dreaming. Not one of the awful dreams about her uncle, fortunately. She'd been dreaming about Benjamin. In her dream he could see. She was reading to him, some long, boring book, and she'd looked up to see him smiling. His sunglasses were on his lap and his eyes were actually focusing on her. *Who are you?* he'd asked.

Nina wasn't sure how she felt about the dream. It was certainly an improvement over her usual dreams, but at the same time it was slightly disturbing in a way. Benjamin had been asking who she was, like he really didn't recognize her, but at the same time there had been this slight leer in his expression.

It wasn't at all like the way she remembered her uncle looking at her, not really. Still, it had made her feel strange. In the dream and now, remembering it.

The dream obviously had some great metaphorical

meaning that she was just too sleepy to make sense of right now. Maybe she'd remember to tell Dr. Kendall next week. Shrinks loved dreams.

She fell back asleep, wondering if it was possible that people met in their dreams, sharing the same dream, or if that was just some dopey romantic idea she'd heard from Zoey.

1:04 A.M.

Jake opened one eye, glued nearly shut by sleep. For a moment, he thought he saw Claire right there in his room. Then he realized it was just a shadow cast on the sheer curtains by the moon. His mouth was parched from the alcohol working its way through his system. He decided to get up and get a drink of water but fell asleep before he could act on the urge.

1:10 A.M.

Lucas drifted through a shockingly explicit dream involving Zoey, a starlit beach, and slow motion. Several times he moaned in his sleep. Finally the sound of his own voice woke him up. He groaned and tried to go immediately back to sleep, hoping to complete the dream. Instead he drifted into a completely uninteresting dream involving cows.

1:45 A.M.

Benjamin pushed the button on the clock and it spoke the time: "The time is one forty-five A.M." He had been awake, lying in his bed for an hour after waking up from a dream. It was one of the "seeing" dreams he'd had often back in the days after he first lost his sight. This time, in the dream, he'd been dreaming he was blind and when he woke, he was relieved to discover that he could see perfectly well.

Then he'd been on the ferry, on a brilliantly sunny day. Many of the people he knew were there: Zoey, Jake, Claire, Nina. And then in the dream he'd realized that it *was* only a dream. The people he was seeing were all as they'd been when he was much younger. A ten-year-old Zoey, a Jake who was still a boy, a Claire in knee socks.

And then a little girl with braces had come over and taken his hand. She had an unlit Lucky Strike dangling from her lip and was carrying some large, boring-looking book. Nina.

I was just dreaming about you, she said.

Benjamin lay back in his bed and tried to forget the visual images. They were meaningless, just part of a dream. The real world was darkness.

2:08 A.M.

Claire smiled in her sleep. She was dreaming of a huge storm, rolling right over the top of the widow's walk while she ate peanuts under her rain slicker.

3:00 A.M.

Christopher's alarm went off, and he woke feeling tired and demoralized. His three hours of sleep had been fitful. He shouldn't have asked Zoey to talk to Aisha. That was so high school. Aisha would think he was being a wimp. She'd think he was crawling

91

back to her, looking for forgiveness. Only he wasn't in the wrong here. He wasn't. If anyone should apologize, it was probably Aisha, only he was too damned tired to think of why.

Well, let it go, he told himself. *Forget about it. Shouldn't have let the girl ruin your sleep.*

He sat up in bed and shook his head, trying to clear away the bad feelings. He had work to do, papers to deliver. Couldn't sleep now. Papers to deliver. Like to Aisha's house.

He got up and made a quick cup of coffee.

4:28 A.M.

Aisha drifted through a shockingly explicit dream involving Christopher, an open bedroom window, and slow motion. Several times she moaned in her sleep. Finally the sound of her own voice woke her up. She looked first at the window. No, it was securely locked.

Then she heard what sounded like footsteps on the frosty pine needles outside, a sound like cornflakes crunching. A moment later, a second sound like a bike on gravel. She went back to sleep, annoyed at her subconscious for concocting ridiculous scenarios involving a guy she had already forgotten.

4:50 A.M.

Nina had another dream. Someone was holding her hand. Or, more accurately, several someones. One minute it was Benjamin. Then it was her uncle. Then, oddly enough, Zoey. Then it was her shrink, who was attaching electrodes. Nina pulled her hand away and stuck it under her pillow.

Nina

Once, like years ago when I was only fourteen and hence not responsible for the sheer dorkiness of my actions, I tried to simulate what Benjamin "saw" of me. I got out my little tape recorder and taped myself chattering away in a sort of _Beverly Hills 90210_ kind of sophisticated conversation, very cool. No, way past cool.

Now, don't laugh too much, because we both know that you've pranced around in front of the mirror making pouting faces and sucking in your stomach and thrusting out your buffers with your hands on your hips, imagining what you look like to some guy. I just had to be more inventive.

Anyway, I played back the tape, while smelling my deodorant, my toothpaste, and my shampoo in a sort of approximation of the input Benjamin got off me.

Okay, maybe that is stranger than pouting in a mirror.

Anyway, I was able to conclude from this experiment that I was probably making a very good impression on Benjamin. Assuming Benjamin liked girls who sounded like Tiffani-Amber Thiessen on speed and reeked of Crest Mint Gel.

I don't think at that point that I had really begun to have romantic thoughts about Benjamin.

He and Claire were just moving into total couplehood then, and I still mostly thought of him as Zoey's mysterious big brother.

In fact, I wasn't sure I even liked him until one day when he and I were in the Passmores' living room, waiting for Zoey for some reason or other. I was kind of at a loss for anything to say because what I really wanted to say was _Hey, if you're blind, can you still pee standing up?_ which, even then, seemed like a fairly idiotic question. Anyway, what I ended up doing was blurting out the whole tape recorder and toothpaste story.

He laughed till I thought he was going to collapse a lung.

Then he said, "Thanks, kid. That was the funniest thing I've heard in weeks."

Not the dumbest thing, or the most pathetic thing, or the strangest thing, which is what Claire, or a lot of my friends, would have said. The funniest. He was actually grateful to me for making him laugh.

I've liked Benjamin ever since.

Nine

Thursday morning was a cold one as Zoey, Nina, and Aisha huddled together on the deck of the ferry. Not Maine-winter cold, which would drive them all belowdecks to the heated comfort zone, but crisp and windy. The water was the color of lead, beneath a sky like the underside of a mattress that stretched from horizon to horizon in unbroken gloom.

Nina was sucking frantically on her unlit cigarette and chattering at a mile a minute. Aisha seemed lost in some private reflection, occasionally smiling dreamily, then scowling as if to compensate. Zoey felt gloomy and distracted, watching Jake hunched forward in one of the last benches, looking sick.

"I don't know," Nina said. "I mean, how do you decide these things? On the one hand, I want to look all right so that people won't think I'm Benjamin's pity date, like *What's he doing with skank-woman?* But I don't want to suddenly turn into you, Zoey; no offense, but you know what I mean. I can't do the J. Crew, Miss Perfect Teen, could-be-a-cheerleader-if-I-really-wanted-to, shop at The Gap, honor society with oak leaf clusters, listen to bands where no one has a tattoo, practically-ready-for-VH1 thing." She sucked on her cigarette and glared at Aisha. "What are you grinning about?"

"Just buy a dress you like," Zoey suggested. "Benjamin's not a person who is hung up on fashion. He doesn't know what fashion is."

"A *dress*. Like you're saying it has to be a *dress*?" Nina asked anxiously.

"I'm not saying that, Nina, although I imagine you'll want to wear a dress. You know, it's not quite the prom, but it's like the number-two dance of the year as far as getting dressed up and all."

"Hey, babe." Lucas dropped into the bench behind them, leaned forward, and squeezed Zoey's shoulders.

"Where have you been?" Zoey asked. "And by the way, I have to talk to you about something. Later."

"That doesn't sound good."

"It's not something we should go into now," Zoey said quietly but significantly. "All I'm going to say is you have to think about whose side you're on when you're keeping secrets."

"You mean—" He jerked his head slightly toward Aisha.

"You know what I mean," Zoey said, nodding discreetly.

"That was a guy thing, Zoey. What was I supposed to do?"

"Can we do this later?" Zoey said.

"What?" Aisha asked, surfacing from her reverie.

"Nothing, Eesh," Zoey said quickly.

"Lucas, you're a guy," Nina said, twisting around in her seat. "You think a girl should be herself more, or do you like it when she gets into the whole show-me-off-to-all-your-guy-friends-so-they-can-see-that-

98

you're-like-enough-of-a-stud-to-get-a-babe-to-go-out-with-you thing?''

Lucas stared at her silently for a minute. ''Could you repeat the question?''

''Please don't ask her to do that,'' Zoey said.

''I don't understand,'' Lucas admitted.

''She's asking for advice on what to wear to the homecoming dance,'' Zoey translated.

''Clothing advice?'' Lucas said, making a face.

''Fortunately, I don't have to worry about what to wear,'' Aisha muttered.

''You can come with Benjamin and me,'' Nina said, grinning. ''If—''

''I know,'' Aisha interrupted. ''If I'm real quiet, he won't even know I'm there.''

''Don't be doing that, Aisha,'' Nina chided. ''Don't jump in and steal my punch lines.''

''GOD, I'M COLD,'' Zoey suddenly exploded. ''Why didn't I wear a coat?''

''Come sit back here with me,'' Lucas suggested. ''I'll warm you up.''

''See, that's the other thing,'' Nina said. ''What am I supposed to do, get some dress that shows major cleave and freeze them off?''

''I'm going to tell you what to do,'' Zoey said, rubbing her arms with her hands. ''Go to the book-store at the mall. Buy the latest *Seventeen* or *YM* and get whatever outfit they have on the cover. Or else some other magazine.''

''*Popular Mechanics,*'' Lucas suggested.

''It's the day after tomorrow,'' Nina said bleakly.

''I wish someone would break my leg between now and then,'' Lucas said, falling into the bad mood. ''I have to play the dork, and not only that, I have to act like I'm really grateful for the honor.''

"I didn't vote for you for homecoming king, by the way," Nina said. "I voted for you for queen."

"Thank you, Nina."

"Don't pretend you're not looking forward to it, Lucas," Zoey said, shivering. "I s-s-saw you with K-burger getting all blushy. You two doing your little slow d-d-dance around the room with the spotlight; you'll probably love it."

Lucas leaned forward and wrapped his arms around Zoey's shoulders. She gratefully accepted the warmth of his body. "It wasn't K-burger I was dreaming about all last night."

Aisha looked up sharply, alert again. "What dream?"

"I don't think we want to hear about Lucas's dream," Zoey said.

"It was a perfectly nice dream," Lucas protested. "You, me, a starlit night. Very romantic."

"Romantic?"

"That's right, romantic. I'd even say it was poetic. What's that word? Lyrical. It was lyrical. Warm, gentle breezes, swaying palm trees, soft music."

"I don't think dreams mean anything, do you?" Aisha asked.

"Sometimes," Nina said.

Zoey shivered again and tucked her chin down into the neck of her sweater. "I hope I was dressed warmly in this dream."

"Well, it *was* a warm night," Lucas said.

"That's what I figured," Zoey muttered. "Aisha? I have to ask you something I've never asked anyone before in my life."

"What?"

"Can I stick my hands in your coat pocket?"

* * *

100

Benjamin shared two classes each day with Claire, first and last period. Calculus in the morning, physics at the end of the day. In both classes they still sat near each other, a holdover from the days when they were a couple. They were the most difficult classes for Benjamin since they each involved endless notations on the chalkboard. Their calc teacher was very good about always explaining verbally what she was writing on the board, but the physics teacher, Mr. Aubrey, tended to mumble and become so involved in scribbling that for Benjamin the class was reduced to the sound of chalk on the board.

This was one of those times, and Benjamin wondered, for the twentieth time since the beginning of the school year, if he hadn't gone a step too far, trying to deal with a physics elective.

Thankfully, he had a superb memory, particularly for all things mathematical, and it was something he had learned to develop even further. All of North Harbor, much of downtown Weymouth, the mall, the school, the individual classrooms existed in his head as neat, precise diagrams measured in numbers of steps.

In addition, he cataloged other clues—the direction of the airflow from fans and heaters in various classrooms; the sound of a fluorescent light that buzzed in the cafeteria and told him whether he was close to the start of the lunch line; even the distinctive breathing of different classmates. For Benjamin, the entire world was a series of remembered clues, assembled into maps he used for navigation.

But keeping all the complexities of physics formulas hanging in his mind, moving them, correcting them, reconfiguring them, all in his mind, was a real challenge. Especially when the teacher was spacing out. It would mean a lot of extra effort, going through the Braille version of the textbook. Unfortunately, Nina wasn't a lot of help in reading math.

The bell rang and Benjamin sighed with relief. He waited for the rush of departing bodies to thin out. He thought he had more or less understood the lesson, but he wasn't sure. He didn't even need it to graduate. He'd only taken it because it was reputedly the hardest class on the curriculum and taking it would show that he wasn't letting anything scare him.

"Sometimes your ego gets out of control, Benny boy," he muttered under his breath.

"Did you say something?"

Claire. The voice, the smell of her hair. "Just mumbling," he said.

"Yeah, you and Mr. Aubrey both," Claire said. "Did you understand any of that?"

"I'll manage it somehow," he said sarcastically.

"That's not what I meant, Benjamin. I wasn't being condescending. I meant *I* didn't understand what he was saying."

"Try it without being able to see the damned board." Benjamin was frustrated and taking it out on Claire, he realized, which wasn't fair. But he wasn't in the mood to be fair.

"It doesn't help," Claire said, showing no sign that his attitude was annoying her. "He writes just like he talks. The man needs a full-time interpreter."

"Really?" Benjamin felt better, despite himself. It was a relief to think that everyone else wasn't blazing right through and only he was failing to keep up. "I'm thinking an extra history class would have been a better choice as an elective," he admitted.

"Physics isn't an elective for me," Claire said glumly. "I have to take it if I'm going to go for the kinds of classes I want in college. The hallway's pretty much clear, by the way."

"Thanks." He started to walk away—four steps along the row of desks, careful for the ones that had been pushed out of line, a right turn, seven steps to the door.

Claire was still beside him. "So."

"So . . . so I guess I'll see you on the ferry," he said.

"Yeah, well, look, since there's no one around right now and there will be on the ferry—"

"Let me guess. Nina."

"I'd almost forgotten your annoying habit of reading minds," Claire said. "Come on. I'll walk you, then you won't have to be counting all the way."

Benjamin felt her take his hand and place it on her arm. Her touch sent a wave of warmth through him. He fought to keep his features impassive.

"First of all," Claire said, "I know you know all this, but I feel like I have to mention it anyway—"

"You're concerned because Nina has just gone through this whole thing with your uncle."

"You know, you might at least let me finish saying something before you guess the end."

"Sorry."

"I am a little worried," Claire admitted.

"Isn't this big-sisterly concern a little unusual for you, Claire?"

"This doesn't fall into the usual sibling rivalry category, Benjamin. What happened to Nina is different." Claire's voice was serious. He could hear the fresh edge of outrage.

"I know."

"We're coming to the stairs," Claire said.

"I know. Four more steps," Benjamin said. He

103

stopped at the top of the stairs. "Look, Claire, you're right, I do know all this, okay? I know you're just trying to be a good sister, for the first time in your life—"

"If I'd been a better sister earlier, maybe I could have done something to help her," Claire said. "I hope that son of a bitch goes to jail and dies there."

Benjamin smiled. "That will be our 'happy thought' for the day."

"Yeah. I hate to wish that on anyone, I guess, but he has it coming. Anyway. Look, Benjamin, all I'm saying is be aware of how much this means to Nina."

"I know, it's her first real date."

"It's more than that. I mean, you do realize she's in love with you, right?"

Benjamin laughed. "No, she just has a crush on me because I'm conveniently nonthreatening."

Claire took both his hands in hers. "No, Benjamin, it's more than that. She's had a crush on you for a long time. As in years. It was no big deal as long as you and I were together and she wasn't at all serious about getting involved with guys, but both of those things have changed."

Benjamin began to feel uneasy. Partly because he didn't like hearing Claire dismiss their relationship almost casually. Maybe she had written it off, but he had not. But he was also uneasy because there was truth in what Claire was saying. Things *had* changed. For Nina as well as for Claire and him.

"So. What is it you're afraid I'll do?"

Claire hesitated. "Don't . . ." She took a deep breath. "Benjamin, you're a very easy person to fall for."

Benjamin's heart tripped at her words and the way she had said them, but he fell back on his usual ironic detachment. "Yeah, a blind guy is every girl's dream. No need to do makeup."

"You're frighteningly smart and perceptive, you listen to people when they talk, you're kind and generous, you have a wonderful sense of humor. You're confident. And I know you always suspect people are lying when they tell you this, but you are also very good-looking. Frankly, if you weren't blind, you'd probably be the most arrogant, full-of-himself, stuck-up jerk in this school." Her voice grew soft. "Believe me, Benjamin, you are very easy to fall in love with."

Benjamin wanted to say something, but for once he was at a loss. He wished Claire hadn't said that last part. They were alone in the hallway of the now nearly deserted school. She was so close he could feel the heat from her body. He so desperately wanted to put out a hand, find her smooth cheek, draw her full lips toward his.

But it was Nina they were talking about.

"I'm just saying, as corny as it sounds, don't break Nina's heart, Benjamin. Don't lead her on if you're not serious."

"It'll be okay, Claire," he said, unable to avoid the bitterness. "I'm easy to fall *out* of love with, too."

He felt her cool fingers stroke the side of his face. "No, you aren't, Benjamin."

She turned away and ran down the steps. Benjamin listened to the sound recede and disappear.

Ten

Christopher waited outside the school for the final bell to ring. He kept out of sight across the street in a recessed doorway and hoped for a good opportunity.

Zoey and Lucas, Aisha and Nina emerged together, which was unfortunate.

But then Aisha and Nina went off in one direction and Zoey and Lucas headed down Mainsail toward the dock and the home-bound ferry. Almost perfect. It would have been nice if Lucas was out of the picture, but the important thing was that Aisha wasn't around. When he was sure Nina and Aisha were gone, he fell into step behind Zoey and Lucas.

The day, which had started out unusually brutal, had warmed up nicely, and the oppressive cloud cover had broken up a little, letting in rays of slanting afternoon sun. Christopher caught up with Zoey after a couple of blocks. She saw him and gave him a guarded but still friendly smile. He pretended to have just noticed her.

"Oh, hi, Zoey. Hey, Lucas. School's out, huh? I guess I lost track of time."

"Yeah, we busted outta that joint," Lucas said, doing a tough-guy gangster voice. "They couldn't hold us."

"Right." Christopher forced a laugh. "Cool. So, uh, heading on down to the ferry, huh?"

"More or less," Lucas said. "What's up with you?"

Christopher shrugged. "Oh, not much. I have a couple hours off. Killing time." He looked at Zoey, then looked away.

"My old man would love you, Christopher," Lucas said. "He thinks people should work twenty-four hours a day."

"Yeah." Again Christopher gave Zoey what he felt was a pretty obvious look.

"Um, Lucas, I think Christopher wants to talk to me about something," Zoey said.

"I'm not stopping him," Lucas said. Then he made eye contact with Zoey. "Oh, you mean like something private."

Zoey smiled and Christopher made a point of staring up at a building, like he was counting the floors.

"Fine. I can take a hint. I'll just . . . I'll just go down to the Green Mountain and get a cup of coffee." He started to walk away. "All by myself."

Christopher realized he hadn't exactly handled everything with the subtlety he'd hoped to pull off. "I was just wondering, Zoey. You know, what we were talking about at work last night. You know."

"Aisha?"

"Yeah, that's it."

Zoey drew him out of the traffic on the sidewalk into the mouth of an alleyway. "I can't be the middleman—or middlewoman—between you two, Christopher," she said sternly. "But she did say she doesn't *hate* you. She's just very disappointed in you. She thought you were better than that, that you meant more to each other than that."

Christopher cringed. Guilt trip. That's what it was, a guilt trip Aisha was laying on him. And he had no reason to feel guilty. No reason.

On the other hand, Aisha had not left his thoughts as easily as he'd hoped. In fact, she kept reappearing frequently. Through the night. While he was trying to get work done. Very frequently. Not that he was ever going to buy into her whole one-on-one-only thing.

But he did miss her. And he wasn't starting to miss her any less.

And it was just barely possible that he really had hurt her feelings and her sense of pride when he'd gotten that Angela girl to come to his room.

"I can't give you advice, all right?" Zoey said. "But it probably wouldn't kill you to say you're sorry."

"Sorry." He tried the word out experimentally.

"What do you think you're doing, boy?"

Christopher froze. He registered a look of shock on Zoey's face. He turned around.

The blow was staggering. He fell straight back, collided with Zoey, then hit the hard concrete of the alley. The second blow he saw coming, a steel-buckled boot that slammed into his stomach, knocking the wind out of him. He gasped for air.

He heard Zoey scream. He heard a harsh voice laughing and taunting him. *Black boy's got a white girl in the alley.* A blow to his kidneys. Searing pain. His vision all red.

"Get the girl," a voice said.

"Let her go," a second voice countered. "Let's take care of nappy here."

Christopher tried to wipe the blood out of his eyes and get a look at his tormentors, but there was yet another blow. He vomited.

108

A sound of running feet.

A girl's voice, sobbing. His head being lifted and pressed against softness. *I wish I could just pass out*, he thought. And then he did.

Eleven

"Down, twenty-one, fourteen, hup, hup!"

Jake saw the center move the ball back between his legs to the quarterback. Jake lunged forward, knocking Tony DeSantos aside, and began to run downfield. He ran ten paces and cut sharply left, turning to see the ball flying through the air. A good, rifled pass, a little high but within easy reach. Jake reached.

The ball flew through his outstretched fingers and hit the dirt five yards away.

"Dammit, McRoyan!"

Jake heard the sound of his coach's voice on the sidelines, an angry whine like a hornet. The practice was not going well.

He headed back toward the line of scrimmage. The quarterback, a fellow senior named Fitzhugh, shook his head. "You want me to just walk downfield and hand it to you next time, McRoyan?"

"You overthrew." Jake pulled off his helmet to wipe the sweat from his brow.

"Bull. Try paying attention next time. I'm not throwing passes just for my own entertainment. I was thinking we'd try to actually win our homecoming game for the first time this century."

Jake put the helmet back on and entered the huddle.

"Okay, third and four," Fitzhugh said. "Let's see if we can run against our own defense. Second chance, big Jake. Get us a first down and we'll all forget that last play."

"Eat me, Fitz," Jake said.

"Break!"

They formed up on the line, facing their fellow teammates, a defense that was known to be weaker than the threat they'd be facing the next night. The team from Bangor was reputed to have several players over two hundred and fifty pounds.

"Down, twenty-one, hup, hup, hup!"

Jake dropped back, spun, ran to meet Fitzhugh, grabbed the ball from his outstretched hand. His foot caught on something. He took two staggering steps, trying to regain his balance, then the express train hit him.

When the laughing defensive lineman finally let him up, he was face to face with the coach. "You want to explain to me what that move was, Mc-Royan?"

"I tripped."

"No kidding. You tripped. Swell. Are you in this practice, McRoyan?"

"Y'sir, Coach," Jake muttered.

"Because I don't think your mind is on football, son. You got your mind on something else? You got your mind on some girl, or what? Because this is a game for people who only have their minds on football. Am I clear on this?"

"Y'sir, Coach."

"We are going to win that game tomorrow night, because I am not going to spend the rest of the season taking crap off every butthole with an opinion in this

111

town, do you read me? Do you *all* read me, loud and clear?''

"Yes, sir," a chorus of masculine voices rang out.

The coach softened just a bit. "Well, they say *bad practice, good game.* By those lights we'll have one hell of a game tomorrow night, because this is one sorry practice. All right, give me some laps and hit the showers."

Jake trotted around the field five times and headed for the locker room, feeling sour and tired. He ignored the good-natured and not-so-good-natured jibes from teammates, showered, and dressed quickly.

Lars Ehrlich fell into step beside him as he made his way across the gym floor and outside into the cool evening. An ambulance was blaring past at high speed in front of the school, red lights flashing crazily off the windows of the buildings.

"You want to bust my ass, too, Lars?" Jake asked without much interest.

Lars shrugged. "Nah. But you did suck out there."

"Yeah, well, you can eat me, too."

"You're hung over, man, that's the problem."

"You know something, Lars, I don't remember when it was you became my mother."

Lars laughed. "I don't give a rat's ass what you do, man. I'm just thinking about the game. We can't win without you."

"Probably can't win *with* me," Jake said. But the mention of the team did strike home. Lars was right. He was part of a team, not just one guy. He couldn't let the team down. Even Fitz, who was a certified jerk. "You heard Coach. Bad practice, good game. We'll do all right."

"Well, maybe tonight would not be a good night to be boozing. Not that I'm your mom."

112

Jake gave him a good-natured shove. "I'll be a real Boy Scout."

"Here." Lars held out his hand, palm down.

"What's that?"

"Just take it," Lars insisted.

Jake held out his hand and a small glass vial dropped into his palm. "Lars, what is this?"

"It's just a little blow, man. No biggie. Do a couple lines before first half, then a couple more for the second half. Instant concentration. You can owe me for it."

"Coke?"

"Oh, don't go all virginal on me, dude. You were sweating like a pig out there. You're out of shape and you're not focusing and I don't want us to lose this game just because you're all screwed up over Claire Geiger."

Jake bristled. "I don't need this crap, Lars."

A police car raced past, apparently following the ambulance toward downtown.

"Okay, then flush it down the toilet. Whatever. But you know, a lot of alumni come back for homecoming, and in case it slipped your mind, the assistant coach from BU is probably going to be at the game. He might take notice of a couple of real hotshot players from his old alma mater. I know your folks are well-off, but my dad's been unemployed for a year, dude. Some athletic scholarship money would help. You hear what I'm saying?"

Jake nodded. "I hear."

"Cool. Later, man."

"Yeah, later."

Twelve

"You know what, Aisha? Maybe you should ask Jake to take you to homecoming," Nina suggested. "I mean, he's not taking Claire . . ."

Aisha shook her head. "Nina, you just love to cause trouble, don't you?"

Nina grinned over the top of her Orange Julius. "I like life to be entertaining."

Aisha looked around her at the mostly empty mall food court. She wasn't about to take up Nina's mischievous suggestion, but it was a reminder that if she wanted to go to homecoming, she had almost no time left to find a date. There was a guy in her calculus class she'd thought about, but when the moment had come to approach him, she'd put it off.

Maybe it was some lingering hope that things would work out with Christopher at the last moment. A hope based on the fact that Zoey said he was asking about her. He wouldn't be asking if he weren't still interested.

"Well, I'm basically done," Nina said, tossing her paper cup toward the trash bin.

"With your drink, or with shopping?"

"Both. I've made a final, irrevocable decision. I'm just going to wear the same dress I wore when Benjamin and I went down to that concert in Portland.''

Aisha rolled her eyes. "In other words, we've just wasted all the time we spent here."

"I bought this," Nina said, holding up a Pearl Jam CD. *"And"*—she fished in a bag and produced a pair of very dark shades—"I got these. Now Benjamin and I will be sort of making a joint fashion statement."

Aisha smiled. "And I got a three-pack of all-cotton underwear. So, I guess this shopping trip was a major success."

Nina started to say something, but Aisha held up her hand. "Shh. Listen."

"To what?"

"The P.A.—shh."

"Oh my God. They're paging *you*," Nina said. "Unless there's another Aisha Gray."

Aisha felt a shiver of fear. It had to be an emergency. She had never heard anyone be paged in the mall before. Her mom had been hurt! Or her dad had had a heart attack! She jumped up. "Where do I go? Where am I supposed to go?"

"Um, um, the um, the information place! That round thing where they give out strollers."

Aisha took off at a near run. Kalif, it could be her brother. Her heart was pounding.

"Eesh, it could be nothing," Nina said hopefully. "Maybe you dropped your wallet and they found it or something."

Aisha spotted the information kiosk and broke into a run. "I'm Aisha Gray, I'm Aisha Gray."

The old woman behind the counter stared at her in annoyance. "Yes, there's a telephone call for you." She punched a button and handed the receiver to Aisha.

115

"Who is this?"

"Aisha?" Zoey's voice, strained and edgy.

"Zoey? What's the matter? Is it my mom?"

"Listen, Aisha, it's Christopher."

Aisha's heart thumped and seemed about ready to stop beating. "Oh my God."

"He's hurt, Aisha." Aisha heard the sob in Zoey's voice and almost dropped the receiver. "We're at County Hospital."

"Is he okay?"

"I don't know yet." A long silence. "There was a lot of blood. I don't know."

Nina slammed on the brakes, and her father's seventy-thousand-dollar Mercedes came to a stop with the front grille just millimeters from the car in front of her.

Aisha was out of the car before it had completely stopped, leaving the door open behind her, running to the big glass doors that opened electronically. She dashed into the crowded emergency room, a cacophony of crying children, Oprah's theme song on the TV, computer printer chatter, and repeated chime tones over the p.a.

She spotted Zoey. Lucas was just beyond her, but what held Aisha's gaze was the drying bloody stain smeared across the front of Zoey's sweater.

"Is he okay? Is he okay?"

Zoey ran to meet her, nodding vigorously and saying, "He's going to be fine, the doctor just came out and said he's going to be fine." Then Zoey was hugging her and Aisha felt like she might faint.

"They said it looked worse than it was. There was all this blood, but he just broke a couple of ribs and he's all swollen and bruised, but he's okay."

116

Aisha realized she was weeping, letting her tears moisten Zoey's hair. "God. What happened? Was he riding his bike?"

Aisha could feel Zoey take a deep, steadying breath. "It wasn't an accident."

Aisha backed away to look at Zoey. "What do you mean? What was it?"

"Some guys beat him up. I think there were three of them." Zoey looked away. "Three white guys."

"Well . . . what . . . I mean, what, why did they beat him up?"

"They—they were skinheads or something."

Aisha felt a cold calm settle over her, blanking out her worry. "You mean they beat him up because he's black?"

"I think so," Zoey said. "We were talking, just the two of us. Lucas was down the street. I think they thought we were together. A black guy and a white girl."

Aisha nodded slowly. "I see."

"There wasn't any warning or anything. It all happened so fast. One second we were talking, then Christopher was on the ground and these guys were kicking him, calling him . . . you know."

Two uniformed policemen stepped out of a room, looking bored. They stopped and surveyed the four of them. "You two are new," the older of the two cops said, indicating Aisha and Nina. "Did either of you witness the incident?"

"No," Nina said. "We were at the mall."

The policeman nodded. "Well, anyone thinks of anything, give us a call. You may be contacted by detectives."

"Are you going to be able to catch the guys?" Zoey asked.

"There's no way to be sure. We don't have a lot of evidence yet. The victim says he never got a clear look at the guys who jumped him. And all you've been able to tell us is that they were white, young skinhead types. But we'll probably catch them sooner or later. These types of perpetrators aren't usually real smart. Sooner or later we'll get them."

Aisha was barely listening after the first few words. She had gone to the door of Christopher's room and was hesitating, her hand on the doorknob. She might be the last person Christopher wanted to see right now.

But then again, he had no one else to look after him.

She opened the door and stifled a gasp. Christopher was lying flat on his back. White bandages were wrapped around his chest, around his left leg and both arms. His head was bandaged, too, and those bandages were stained with seeping blood. There was a needle stuck into his arm at the elbow, attached by a long plastic tube to a clear pouch that hung overhead.

She moved closer and saw that his face was a mass of swelling. His left eye was swollen completely shut and the lid bristled with stitches. There were more stitches above his lips and just around the bottom of his ear.

When he spoke, his voice was a hoarse whisper, barely intelligible. "I look like hell, don't I?"

Aisha shook her head and fought unsuccessfully to hold back the tears. She sought a place where she could touch him, make some sort of physical contact, and found an undamaged patch on his shoulder.

"Does it hurt a lot?"

"Mmm. They were . . . stoned on all kinds of stuff. Doesn't hurt. Later, yeah."

"The doctor told Zoey you're going to be all right."

"Until . . . the bill," he said, trying feebly to laugh.

"Oh, God, Christopher."

"I'm fine, Eesh . . . cry. Don't cry."

"I'm sorry, I can't help it."

"Look, nurse will . . . kick you out, so I need you to . . ."

Aisha leaned closer so he wouldn't have to strain as much to make himself heard. He smelled of antiseptic and Vaseline. "Anything. I'll do anything."

"Make sure . . . Mr. Passmore knows . . . can't work tonight. Also, school . . . tell Coach. And the papers . . . Oh, damn . . ."

Aisha almost laughed. Typical Christopher. She'd been expecting something personal, and what he was worried about was his work. "I could deliver your papers," she said.

"No—"

"Sure I can. Do you have some kind of a list somewhere? In your apartment?"

"Late."

"I know. I'll just sleep through some classes."

He tried to nod, but the effort obviously hurt.

"Don't move. And don't worry, I'll take care of everything for you. And when they let you go, you can come stay at my house. We have plenty of rooms and they're all vacant, no customers. You could have your own Jacuzzi and silk sheets and all."

His eyelids drifted down. "That . . . last shot . . . made me kind of sleepy."

"Go ahead and sleep. Sleep as much as you can." She stroked his shoulder tentatively.

"Aisha?"

"Yes, I'm still here."

"Sorry."

"It's not your fault you're in here," Aisha blazed.

"No." He tried his fractured smile again. "Sorry. You know."

"Go to sleep," she whispered.

Thirteen

By the time they left the hospital, it was after eight o'clock. They walked in a group down toward the ferry landing, unable to think of anything else to do, even though it was more than an hour's wait for the next ferry.

Zoey tried to make conversation with Aisha, but she had withdrawn into herself, silent, barely making eye contact with her friends. Nina, as always when she was in a serious situation, had very little to say.

Lucas was nearly as distant as Aisha, sullen, almost seething.

Zoey led the way to the Green Mountain, a coffee shop where the smell of fresh-roasted coffee and homemade cookies filled the air. They found a small table. Zoey had tea. Lucas and Nina had coffee. Aisha just sat.

"You should have something," Zoey suggested.

"No thanks."

"It might make you feel better."

"I don't want to feel better," Aisha erupted suddenly, the first sign of emotion since she had emerged from Christopher's room.

"He's going to be fine," Zoey said. "He's in great shape; you always said so, remember?"

"Just leave me be, Zoey," Aisha said bitterly.

Zoey felt annoyed. More than annoyed, she had quite quickly become very angry. Christopher's blood still caked the front of her sweater and now she wore Lucas's jacket to cover the mess. "Aisha, Christopher is my friend, too. He's our friend."

"He didn't get beaten up for being your friend," Aisha snapped. "He got beaten up for being black."

"What's that supposed to mean?" Zoey said sharply.

"It means what it means. All right? It means what it means."

"It wasn't *my* fault he got hurt, dammit."

"It's all your faults. All of you." Aisha's voice was rising to a furious shout. "You were standing right there, but oh, no, you can't give any kind of description. But I'll bet if they were black guys, you'd have remembered. Damn right you would."

"You think I would protect those creeps?" Zoey shouted. She had never been so angry. It was like a volcano erupting inside her.

"The only reason this happened was because he was with you. Because he was with a white girl."

"You asked me to talk to him!"

"Why didn't you try and tell those bastards he was your friend; did you even try that?"

"Screw you, Aisha. You weren't there. All right?"

"Yeah, and you were, and your white boyfriend and a lot of other white people and all of you did nothing because it was just one more black kid getting what he deserved."

"Shut up! Shut up! You're so full of crap, Aisha— you know that's a lie!"

Lucas put a hand forcefully on Zoey's shoulder and pulled her back into her chair. She hadn't even realized that she had lunged forward. She was trembling. She felt nauseous. She felt like screaming at the top of her lungs and breaking things.

Aisha shoved her chair back with a loud scrape and started to leave. Nina stood in her way.

"Chill, Eesh," Nina said.

"Both of you," Lucas said. "Sit down, Aisha."

Zoey realized the room had fallen silent. All eyes were surreptitiously watching them. The manager of the place had stepped from behind the counter, like he was gearing up for trouble.

"Come on, Aisha," Lucas said in a calm voice.

Aisha hesitated, looking mad enough to start throwing punches, but at last she sat down.

"Look, you're both just upset," Lucas said. "It's normal. It's what happens when you're this close to violence. Believe me, I've seen more violence probably than either of you. You're just reacting."

"Come on," Nina added. "You two aren't mad at each other. You're mad at the guys who hurt Christopher."

Zoey forced herself to take several deep breaths. Her shoulder muscles were painfully knotted. Her hands were shaking.

"If I could, I'd kill them," Aisha snarled.

"I wish I had seen them," Zoey said, a tear running down her cheek. "I'm sorry. I was just scared and it happened so fast and I was screaming and trying to get help."

Aisha nodded grudgingly. "It's not your fault."

"I didn't know what to do," Zoey said bleakly. "I was really scared."

"I have to get some air," Aisha said. She stood up again. "I'll see you guys on the ferry."

Zoey started to protest, but she felt too weary to argue any more.

"I better go keep an eye on her," Lucas said. "Those guys may still be out there looking for trouble."

"Those guys?" Nina asked. "Do you know who they are?"

"No. No, I just meant guys like that. Guys like those may still be out on the streets."

He went after Aisha. Zoey let her head sink down onto the table. She had the feeling she had missed something important, but the truth was, she was just too tired to care.

Lucas kissed Zoey good night at her front door. Neither of them was up for much more just then. He took the path behind her house up to his own home, skirting below the overhanging deck that was his home's only adornment. His father had added it because it gave a good view of the harbor, and more specifically of the lobster boat that was his livelihood.

Lucas had missed dinner, not that either of his parents cared one way or the other. His mother was in the kitchen, washing dishes. His father was already up in his room, getting ready to go to bed. Mr. Cabral kept very early hours, always heading down to the boat before dawn.

"You want something to eat, Lucas?" his mother asked.

She was a faded, worn woman, going through the motions of life, cooking, cleaning, attending church, sewing little doilies that decorated the backs and arms of all the clean but shabby furniture.

When he was a little boy, Lucas had tried to engage her, cheer her up, make her laugh. She had been uninterested, showing no more pleasure in his good behavior than she showed grief at his later petty criminality. She barely existed, Lucas knew. She wasn't really a person at all, just a subset of her husband. In this house it was his father, Roy Cabral, who was the only power.

"I'm not hungry," Lucas said.

"It's in the refrigerator if you want some later. Pot roast."

"Okay, Mom."

"How was school?"

Lucas smiled. "School was fine." There was no point in telling her that what happened after school had not been so fine. This was hardly a liberal household. Neither of his parents would much care if a black guy minding his own damned business got the crap beaten out of him. After all, they didn't subscribe to any of the papers Christopher delivered.

Lucas went upstairs to his spare, functional room and flopped back on the bed. He shut his eyes, and inevitably the images were of Christopher lying delirious on the ground, and of Zoey cradling his bloody head.

Snake's work, he knew. And his pal Jones, and some other guy Lucas hadn't recognized. Typical skinhead treatment—three guys against one. Even that was bold for them. Normally they'd have wanted the balance even more in their favor. Probably they were drunk or high on crack.

He had nearly screwed up and blurted the truth to Zoey, which would have been a disaster. If she knew he could identify the perpetrators by name, Zoey would insist he tell the cops.

He wasn't going to do that. If he ended up testifying in court, there was every possibility that Snake

125

and his skinhead friends would try to retaliate. Lucas wasn't worried for himself. He still had the self-preserving alertness that had served him well in the Youth Authority. But Zoey was another matter.

What the skins had done to Christopher was sickening, the product of marginal humans with below-borderline IQs and families so screwed up they made his home life look like a Hallmark commercial. But Lucas wasn't going to turn Christopher's problem into Zoey's problem.

Fourteen

Aisha rarely drove her parents' island car, and she had never before driven it around at three o'clock in the morning. Fortunately, the ancient AMC Pacer had a decent muffler, unlike most other island cars. It had no front or rear bumpers, and the left window was a sheet of plastic held on by duct tape, but it did have a muffler, so the noise as she crept along dark streets toward the dock was minimal.

No one wasted money on a car useful only for driving to and from the ferry to carry groceries. *Real* cars were kept on the mainland in parking garages. In fact, it was almost a mark of pride among Chatham Islanders, whatever their social status, to be able to brag about having the worst, most rusted out, battered piece of junk on the island.

Aisha pulled the car to a stop announced by loudly squealing brakes. She yanked on the door release and slammed the door with her shoulder. It opened just enough for her to be able to squeeze out by using tricks a contortionist would have envied.

The dock was empty, lit by two globes casting lugubrious bluish light over the pilings. The first ferry of the day would not arrive for almost four hours.

Even the early fishermen and lobstermen wouldn't be up for another hour and a half.

It was chilly enough to turn her breath to steam, but there was no wind. The water sloshed wearily against the pilings. A sleepy gull looked her over and dismissed her.

Aisha saw the plastic-wrapped papers, four piles sitting on the siding, glistening with frost. She grabbed the two smallest bundles and dragged them back to the car. Then she went back for the remaining papers. It was unbelievable to think that Christopher delivered all these papers by bike, pedaling all this weight up the long slope to her house.

No wonder he had such a nice, hard little butt. Not that she cared. Or maybe she did. Her feelings were a mess right now. The fact that he had been hurt did not automatically resolve all the problems they had. It would be naive to think that he would suddenly be willing to accept her terms for their relationship.

Aisha heard a sound, a squeaky door closing, and looked around. At first she could see nothing, then she saw a figure approaching from the direction of Passmores', a figure wreathed in steam.

Zoey arrived carrying two Styrofoam cups of coffee, waitress-style, both in one hand. Her other hand held a pastry box.

"What the hell are you doing here, Zoey?" Aisha demanded, not sure whether she was annoyed or amused.

"Same as you. I'm going to help deliver Christopher's papers. I've been waiting over in the restaurant. Here. It's fresh. I hope cream is okay."

She handed Aisha one of the coffees.

"Zoey, you don't have to do this, all right?"

"Eesh, what are you going to do? Crawl in and out

of that broken car door at every stop? It would take you a week. You drive, I'll throw.''

"I can handle it. Christopher is *my* boyfriend. At least he was.''

"Look, Aisha, I know you want someone to be mad at over this, and since we don't have the guys who did it, you're being mad at me. That's fine, you can be mad at me if you want. I'm not leaving.''

Aisha reluctantly took the coffee. She took a sip. "What's in the box?''

"Danish. One cherry, one apple. Cherry's mine. Shouldn't we put rubber bands around these papers or something?''

Aisha produced a big box of narrow plastic bags. She had found them when she went through Christopher's apartment, looking for his delivery list. "I'm not really mad at you, Zoey.'' She sat her coffee on the hood of the car, rolled a *Weymouth Times* and stuffed it into a bag. "I'm just mad, period. For some stupid reason I thought this kind of b.s. was something I left behind in Boston.''

"You told me about your school bus getting turned over down there,'' Zoey said. She began to roll *Portland Press-Heralds*.

"That was just the most dramatic moment,'' Aisha said. "People think racists are only in the old South and that's not true. Try being black and moving into most parts of South Boston. You'll think you were in Alabama.'' She shrugged. "I just thought things might not be that way here in Maine.''

"They aren't that way here,'' Zoey said. "Not with most people, or even very many people.''

Aisha smiled grimly. "Sure they are, Zoey. They're that way everywhere. I don't mean you or Nina or Claire, but still, lots of people. And see, I've had it so easy here on this island that it's like I forgot what the real world was like. It's like I was becoming white, forgetting who I really am. Today . . . yesterday, I guess, now. Anyway, it was wake-up time."

Zoey looked sad. "I guess there are creeps everywhere."

"Yeah, well, I had managed to convince myself that wasn't true. But the fact is wherever I go, and whatever I do or become or accomplish, there are a certain number of white people who will never see anything but a nigger. That's the fact, Zo. A fact for me and a fact for Christopher."

"Well, the facts suck, then."

"I'm not thrilled about them, either."

They worked in silence for several minutes, until all the papers were bagged.

"Sometimes things do get better," Zoey said hopefully. "I mean, we don't burn witches anymore or have slaves or put people in prison for owing money."

Aisha smiled. Zoey was nothing if not an optimist. She had unchallengeable faith in the future. She thought the future would be like *Star Trek*—black and white, even humans and nonhumans getting along and solving all their problems with a few adjustments to the warp engines.

Aisha had learned to be more cautious. She believed in what she saw and experienced, and a fair amount of that had been bad. Not all, but enough. Faith that the world would someday be perfect just seemed naive, especially when Christopher was lying in a hospital in a far-from-perfect world.

"I know you feel bad about what happened to Christopher," Aisha said. "And I was wrong to blame you just because you're white. I take that back.

But it's not all as simple as you think it is. See, I'm as smart as you are, Zoey, maybe smarter in some subjects. I guess I'm more or less as pretty as you are. I can work as hard as you do, I can deal with people as well as you do, I even come from a family that's not much different from yours. And what you think is *Hey, Aisha and I are friends, we're mostly the same, what's the big problem?*"

"We are mostly the same," Zoey said earnestly. "You and I are more alike than I'm like Claire, for example. We're more alike than you and Nina."

"Only we're not. No one will ever call you a nigger, Zoey, or tell you to get out of town and go back to the ghetto where you belong. And no one is ever going to refuse you a chance or a job or whatever because you're the wrong shade. Cops aren't going to pull you over because you look suspicious driving a nice car, or . . . or treat you like you must be a shoplifter every time you walk through a department store. That's a big difference between you and me, Zo. It's not your fault, I know you're not racist, but just the same it's hard for me not to resent it sometimes when it's like the whole damned world is ready to open up to the lovely, lily-white Ms. Zoey Passmore but just waiting for the right time to try and step on the lovely, ebony Ms. Aisha Gray."

Zoey nodded silently. There were tears in her eyes. "I do know all that, Aisha. Really. I just don't know what I can do about all those things."

"Neither do I," Aisha admitted. "Wait for the human race to grow up, I guess, like I could live that long."

"In the meantime, I still want to be your friend."

Aisha sighed. She took Zoey's hand and squeezed

Nina

I was always fascinated by other people's love lives. When Zoey kissed some guy, or Claire did, that didn't set off any of the alarms inside me. It wasn't about _me_, so it was safe. When guys were interested in me, and yes, there were a few, _that_ was different. The first time a male had shown any interest in me it had turned out pretty badly. The memory of those events intruded anytime a guy so much as smiled at me. It was like once, when I was little, I found a worm in a peach. _Half_ a worm, actually.

I will pause a moment while

· you grasp the full meaning of that fact.

For a long time after that I would not eat peaches. But it didn't bother me if someone else ate peaches. In fact, it sort of fascinated me, because underneath it all I had the normal amount of interest in peaches. I mean, I knew the difference between a good-looking peach and a skanky peach. And there were plenty of times when I'd get a sort of internal quiver, a little warmth, a little urge to have a peach, but the memory of the worm kept getting in the way.

Am I being too metaphorical?

Anyway. I'd ask Zoey what it

was like when she'd make out
with Jake, and the one time she
kissed Tad Crowley at a party, and
later with Lucas. And Zoey being
Zoey, her version of events involved words like "wonderful" and
"exciting" and "amazing." Even "tran-
scendent" once. Words that don't
really convey much hard information.

So, like a dolt, I asked Claire
and caught her in a rare helpful
mood. She only rolled her eyes
once, and made no more than half a
dozen smart-ass remarks at my
expense. Then she explained making
out with a guy you really like.

She said the entire rest of
the world just ceases to exist.

You don't see, you don't hear, you don't breathe, you don't think, you don't remember.

Then you stop, and the world comes rushing back in. And that's no fun, so you start up again.

It was the exact opposite of what I felt. For me the very thought of kissing a boy was nauseating, a swirl of guilt and self-hatred and fear. I didn't see any way that my feelings would ever become like Claire's and Zoey's and Aisha's feelings.

And yet, I had hope.

Actually, I have started eating peaches again.

Fifteen

Benjamin woke to Mozart's Symphony Number Forty, having programmed his CD player the night before. The music carried through on the speakers in his bathroom, clearly audible as he showered, shaved, deodorized, and combed his hair.

"Why," he asked his invisible reflection in the bathroom mirror, "would a girl who likes Pearl Jam and the Red Hot Chili Peppers want to go out with a guy who likes Mozart?"

"Why?" he asked, sticking a toothbrush in his mouth, "wou a gir who ever even goes ou choose e?"

He quickly finished brushing, then answered his own question. "I'll tell you why, Bat Boy—because you're safe. You're nonthreatening. Story of your life, man."

He located and put on underwear, a shirt, hopefully white if his mother had put it in the right part of his closet, a pair of pants, definitely denim, and a pullover. Color unknown, but once described by Zoey as "something that would go with anything." Good enough.

A jacket. It would be cold at the game tonight. The leather jacket. He didn't mind being nonthreatening, but a little macho wouldn't hurt. Would it?

Jeez, this was going to be so different from going out with Claire. Claire wasn't exactly a tender, easily bruised flower. It would take a baseball bat to bruise Claire.

Nina was different. Not that she wasn't tough in her own way, but there was this big, unhealed wound on her soul. She was vulnerable. This was a big thing for her, going out with him. Probably Claire had been exaggerating in saying that Nina was in love with him, that was too much, but she *was* sort of putting herself on the line in a way that Claire never did.

"I guess she has a right to start off with someone safe," Benjamin said thoughtfully. "Although . . . I *am* wearing leather. I don't know what color leather it is, but it's manly just the same." He laughed and headed out to the hallway.

"Zoey! You ready?" he yelled upstairs.

Zoey came clattering down the stairs. "Here I am. Ready?"

"Ready."

"Bye, Mom!" Zoey yelled.

"Bye, you two," their mother called from the kitchen.

Outside the air was brisk, but Benjamin felt direct sunlight on his face. It was clear, or at least not completely cloudy. They set off at a walk, Benjamin keeping the count of his steps almost unconsciously as he swung his cane from side to side in a narrow arc.

"I cannot wake up," Zoey complained.

"That's what you get for going out in the middle of the night."

"Sorry, did I wake you up?"

"Nah. I hear everything, you know that. What did you do, go deliver Christopher's papers?"

"Aisha and I, yeah. Thank God it's Friday."

"Mmm. Big night tonight." Benjamin smiled. "How is Lucas doing with the homecoming king deal?"

Zoey laughed. "You'd never guess that being popular and well liked could piss someone off so much."

His sister shifted into her ever-so-casual voice. "So, tonight I guess you're taking Nina to the game."

"Uh-huh. You know how I love listening to football. The crowd murmurs, the crowd starts yelling, there's the sound of a loud crunch from the field, the crowd sighs heavily. Almost as fun as tennis. Thock, thock, thock, thock, crowd groans, then one of the players starts yelling, 'That was in; what are you, blind?' "

"Maybe Nina can describe the game to you," Zoey said, still in her overly casual voice.

"Well, we'll probably be busy making love under the seats," Benjamin said. Zoey was being subtle, which wasn't her greatest talent.

"Very funny."

"That was where you were heading, wasn't it? A few well-chosen words about not doing anything to upset Nina; after all, she's in a sort of vulnerable condition right now? Claire already gave me that line. Jeez, what do you people think I am? The ruthless despoiler of virgins?"

"Of course not," Zoey said. Now she sounded embarrassed. "It's just she's my friend, and you're my brother, and I want it all to work out so there aren't any major conflicts."

"Look, she's going out with me precisely because I'm safe. I mean, come on. I grope in slow motion. I can't kiss anyone without directions from ground control to guide me in. We'll do the thing tonight, we'll do the dance tomorrow night, she'll probably decide it was dull and get on with her life.''

"Is that what you think? That you're just a sort of tryout for her?"

"Training wheels. That's my role in life. For someone like Nina, I'm a safe place to start. For someone like Claire, I'm more a curiosity, a unique experience so that someday she can say *Oh, yes, I've had them all. Why, I even had a blind guy once.*"

"I don't believe I'm hearing self-pity from you."

Benjamin stopped and did a sort of double take. "Damn. You're right. Slap me if I do that again."

They resumed their progress. Benjamin was still disturbed that he had given vent to what sounded a lot like bitterness. That was the wrong attitude. Yes, he'd gotten dumped. But in the same week Claire had dumped him, Zoey had dumped Jake. These things happened to everyone. Especially lately.

"Anyway, I'm just saying that underneath Nina's abrasive and occasionally weird exterior there is a very sweet girl, so don't be fooled."

"Uh-huh. Got it. By the way, what little advice did you give her about me, Mom?"

Zoey laughed. "I told her that underneath your abrasive and occasionally weird exterior there was an abrasive and occasionally weird interior, so she shouldn't be fooled by your nice guy act."

Sixteen

Lucas stood on the grass at the far end of the field and watched the early part of the homecoming game with a sense of impending doom. Not just because the Weymouth team was being beaten by the team from Bangor. Frankly, he didn't really care who won. Inasmuch as he was at all interested in football, it was an abstract interest, not tied to any one team.

But as each play went by, the moment drew nearer.

He had already seen the suit—a white tuxedo. Each of the five candidates for homecoming king had been supplied with a white tuxedo, rented for the occasion and currently hanging in the boys' locker room. They'd be a little chorus line of Barry Manilows.

He was standing behind the opposing team's goalpost, idly wondering why Jake was playing such lousy ball. He was probably burned over the white tuxedos, too, since he also was one of the nominees. Tad Crowley, a third candidate, was standing nearby, smoking marijuana and admiring the distant legs of the cheerleaders.

It was a cool, almost cold night. Thermoses were in heavy use in bleachers packed with students, parents, alumni, and those other members of the local population who lacked meaningful lives.

141

At halftime Lucas, Tad, Jake, and the other two male candidates were due to march out onto the football field wearing the white tuxedos. They would be joined by the five female candidates. The big announcement of the king and queen, already known to everyone in the school, would be made by the principal.

The moment when his name was read out over the p.a. would be the most embarrassing moment of his life. Worse than the strip search when he'd entered the Youth Authority.

Zoey and the female candidates were already in the girls' locker room doing their hair and whatever else it was girls did to get ready.

On the field, Jake went out for a pass. The ball sailed through his fingers.

"I think we're getting our butts kicked," Lucas remarked.

Tad sucked in smoke, and in an I'm-holding-my-breath voice said, "You think Maddie's a real redhead?"

The gun popped, ending the first half, and the team, muddy and dispirited, began to trot across the field in their direction, aiming for the locker room to be berated by their coach.

Lucas cursed. With a sigh, he headed toward the gym. Tad put the joint out on the bottom of his shoe and fell into step beside him.

"Do I look high?" Tad asked.

"Red, unfocused eyes, idiot grin? No, no one would ever guess."

The vanguard of the team passed by across the grass at a jog, slinging their helmets and muttering.

Jake separated himself from them and slowed to fall in with Lucas and Tad. Jake and Lucas had been

142

bitter enemies back before Jake had discovered the truth about the night his brother was killed. And even afterward, there was the fact that Lucas had, by some interpretations, stolen Zoey away from Jake. Recently the two of them had managed to remain polite, but not exactly close to each other.

Jake was muddy and sweating. He looked distracted.

"What's up, big Jake?" Tad asked.

"We're down twenty-seven to seven," Jake said grimly. "Haven't you been watching the game? Or did you just decide you couldn't stand it anymore?"

"I was watching the cheerleaders," Tad admitted.

"They might be the ones playing in the next half," Jake said. "I suck tonight."

"I doubt it's all your fault," Lucas said mildly.

Jake pointed angrily at his teammates, now a dozen yards away. "Tell them that. They're putting the whole thing on me."

"It's this damned dress-up monkey show," Lucas said. "Get that over with and you'll be set for the next half."

"Pathetic," Jake said. It was clear he was referring to himself.

Lucas didn't know how to respond, so he kept quiet.

After the darkness they had traversed from the football field, the fluorescence through the back door of the locker room was blinding.

Jake went straight to the showers, ignoring his dirty, depressed teammates and their occasional sullen barbs. Lucas sighed and picked up the plastic-sheathed tuxedo, shaking his head in disgust.

"By the way, I will have to kill the first person

143

who gives me any crap about this," he said in a conversational tone.

He undressed down to his underwear and pulled on the slick, cold tuxedo pants. "Oh, man," he complained. "These things are about two sizes too big around the waist."

"That's so K-burger can fit in there with you tomorrow night at the dance," one of the football players said. He got a high five for his wit.

"Let's not get into tomorrow night," Lucas said. "One disaster at a time. Besides, this is it for the tux. Tomorrow night I think I'll dress myself."

Jake had toweled off and opened his locker. Lucas saw him look around quickly, then bend over, sticking his head and one hand into the locker. There followed a sharp snorting sound. Then another. Jake emerged, wiping his nose.

"I must have a cold," he told Lucas.

"Yeah, it's going around," Lucas said, playing along with Jake's lie. It wasn't any of his business if Jake was doing coke. It was amazing, given what he knew about Jake, but it wasn't Lucas's problem.

It was also ironic, Lucas realized. He was the one who had just been released from jail, and he was going to walk out on the field perfectly straight, flanked by one guy who was stoned and another guy who was high.

"This younger generation," he said to himself. "What's the world coming to?"

Zoey and the other four girls had to take off their high heels and walk barefoot across the gym floor. Upon reaching the door to the outside, they used each other as supports while they put the heels back on. Then they waited for the white convertibles that were

144

to pick them up and sweep them in semiregal splendor around the football field.

"So where are the guys?" Louise Kronenberger asked. "I can't believe we have to wait for them."

"Yeah, *you* never keep guys waiting," Kay Appleton said, with a wink at Zoey. "Any guys."

"Was that a subtly snide remark?" Louise asked.

Not all that subtle, Zoey thought. "We're going to freeze to death out there. Bare shoulders and a plunging neckline in October? Maybe in Florida."

"Maybe Lucas can warm you up on the way out there," Louise suggested. "He looks like a guy who could warm someone up."

Zoey seethed, but was determined not to show it. Louise was one of those girls who enjoyed making other girls feel insecure. Probably she had a really bad self-image and had to try to compensate, Zoey told herself.

Psychobabble could be such a comfort sometimes.

"He does know how to dance, doesn't he?" Louise asked. "I mean slow dance. You know, where to put his hands on the girl's body, how to move around?"

"I wouldn't know," Zoey said through chattering teeth.

"It seems to me they used to give the girls little fur things to wear over their shoulders," Kay said.

"Not politically correct. Fur is dead," Zoey explained. "And I guess flannel just wouldn't work with the image."

The door opened and Jake was the first one out, snapping his fingers, bobbing his head and looking like he was ready to go. "Ladies, ladies, and more ladies," he said. "You all look beautiful. Even you, Zoey; no hard feelings, you always did look great,

145

Lucas is a lucky guy. Marie, Amelia, Kay, you're hot. Louise, as always.''

"You're in a good mood," Kay said dryly. "Twenty-seven to seven. Just think how happy you'd be if it was fifty-seven to seven."

"We'll be back in the second half," Jake said. "Don't worry, no problem, big Jake has the situation totally under control. I've just been dogging it so that the last-minute comeback will be even more amazing."

Lucas and the rest of the guys came out, most looking content enough. Lucas was scowling.

"Somehow I feel you got me into this," Lucas accused Zoey.

"Wasn't me," Zoey said.

"It was Aisha," Lucas said darkly. "She denies it, but this is all her fault. She should at least be here to see what she's done."

"She's in the stands with Nina and Claire and Benjamin," Zoey said. She smiled and fluttered her eyelashes. "I asked her to take some pictures. Who knows when I'll see you dressed up again?"

"Any word on Christopher?"

Zoey's face fell. "Aisha said he was much better, but she wasn't able to spend much time with him. He was still dopey."

Lucas gave her a significant look and then directed his gaze at Jake. "He's not the only one."

Zoey stared at Jake. He was flirting happily with Louise as though he didn't have a care in the world, laughing at her jokes as well as his own.

The white convertibles pulled up in a long procession. Zoey had been scheduled to drive out to the field with Tad Crowley. She pulled Kay aside. "Do you

146

mind if we switch and I drive out with Jake? He's being a little weird."

"What are you doing?" Lucas asked suspiciously.

"Jake doesn't use drugs," Zoey explained under her breath. "I just want to see if he's all right."

"Zoey, trust me. I spent two years living with every kind of druggie known to man. The boy's buzzed."

Zoey began to argue, but it was time to get going. She climbed into the car, arranging herself precariously on the top of the backseat with her feet resting on the leather cushions.

Jake hopped in beside her, still grinning and tossing lines at Louise, Lucas, and everyone else within hearing.

The car took off, adding a stiff breeze to Zoey's chill. Her arms were goose bumps. Her teeth were literally chattering. "It's f-freezing out here," she said.

Jake shrugged. "It's not bad. You cold? Here, you want my jacket? I can still loan you my jacket, right, without Lucas getting all bent and thinking I'm like trying to get you back? Although you do look good in that dress, I have to admit. Showing leg through the slit, with the heels. And the cleave and all."

"Jake," Zoey said through her shivering, "I don't *have* any cleavage. You're mistaking me for Claire. And as for this dress—"

"Claire's not so hot," Jake said in his new, rapid-fire way. "She thinks she is. I mean, a lot of people, especially guys, think she is. But she's not. I'm not saying anything bad about her or anything, but underneath it all she's just a cold, selfish person. She doesn't care. She thinks she can get away with anything and like everyone is just supposed to go *Oh, it's all right, it's Claire, so we just have to forgive and forget.* See, because it's Claire and everyone thinks she's this . . . this, I don't know.''

"Jake? Are you . . . all right?''

"To tell you the truth, Zo, I'm great. I know I sucked in the first half, but I'm stoked for the big comeback. Stoked.''

"Stoked on what?'' Zoey asked.

Jake cracked his knuckles and slapped his hands together. "Get this little thing over with and boom. Back in the game. I'm so good I could even catch Fitz's lousy passes. You watch. Is Claire here, even?''

"Yes. She's with Nina and Eesh and Benjamin.''

"I know, everyone thinks I lost it first half, but don't give up on me yet. Hundred-yard game, and almost all of it in the second half. Cool. Count on it.''

Zoey turned and looked back at the car behind them. They were just coming under the brilliant stadium lights, and cheers were going up from the onlookers. A pothole sent her lurching and she grabbed Jake's shoulder for support. Glancing back again, she caught a cool, dubious look from Lucas.

Suddenly Jake stared at her, hard, some idea lighting up his eyes.

"What?'' she asked him.

He smiled. "You know something? This is what we'll remember when we get old.''

"Is it?'' She smiled. "I guess it's one of the things we'll remember.''

He nodded. "Yeah. I always figured homecoming would be you and me. Prom the same thing. You and me, Zoey. You and me and I'd gain a hundred yards or more and be the big hero. It's okay, though. Things change. Onward and upward, right?''

* * *

"And hee-e-e-ere they come," Nina announced. She laughed and nudged Aisha. "Zoey must be freezing her cheechees off." For the benefit of Benjamin, who was on her right side, she elaborated. "Picture five white convertibles coming across the field. A guy and a girl in each, along with the drivers who, judging by the little red hats, are all Shriners. Our proud male candidates are in ill-fitting, Las Vegas white tuxedos with powder-blue cummerbunds. Girls in powder-blue gowns, long, glittering, slit up one leg and down the chest. Very Miss America. Jake is waving like he's running for senator. Lucas looks like he may make a run for it at any moment. Zoey is turning a deeper shade of blue than her dress."

Nina was delighted to hear Benjamin laugh. The stands were crowded and they had been forced close together. Her leg was actually touching his, and she was finding she enjoyed the contact. In fact, she was feeling almost giddy. If Claire hadn't been sitting just beyond Aisha, Nina might even have gone all the way and tried to hold his hand. Or not. But in this environment, with everyone bundled up in the great outdoors, everything seemed safe.

"We're having a minor problem," Nina said. "The car exhausts are steaming so much it's like someone turned on a smoke machine. Steaming cars, steaming breath, steaming cups of coffee all around in the stands, the stadium lights turning everyone gray, and here's Mr. Hardcastle to make the big announcement."

"The announcement everyone already knows," Benjamin observed. "I like this. It sort of crystallizes the whole school experience—a series of surreal, semimystical rituals that no one understands, that very few people care about, and that always involve ele-

149

ments of embarrassment and discomfort.''

"These are supposed to be the best years of our lives," Aisha said.

"God, I hope not," Nina heard Claire mutter.

"At least you guys are all seniors," Nina said. "It will be over for you soon. I'll still be trapped here in bizzaro world for an extra year."

"You're all looking at it the wrong way," Benjamin said. "High school never goes away. Stupid teachers become stupid professors become stupid bosses. One set of inexplicable rules and regulations gets traded for another set. Cramped, stuffy classrooms become cramped, stuffy offices. Face it. There's no escape."

"I'll be killing myself now," Nina said.

"You're being awfully philosophical tonight," Claire said.

"I may have eaten too many Jolly Ranchers," Benjamin said with a sly grin. "Sugar depression."

On the field, Mr. Hardcastle was using the word *tradition* for the tenth time in three minutes. He began introducing alumni from the stands. A guy who had graduated in 1959 and now owned a string of oil and lube shops. An old woman who had graduated some time during the Jurassic period and was now the style editor for the newspaper.

"Too bad Christopher had to miss all this magnificence," Nina said.

Aisha smiled. "I guess being in the hospital isn't all bad."

"When's he going to bust out of there?"

"He's getting out Sunday, although he won't exactly be doing cartwheels for a while."

"Damn," Nina said. "And I know how he loves cartwheels. I can help you guys do his papers tonight.

150

Claire will help, too. Isn't that right, Claire?"

Claire nodded glumly.

"I'll drive," Benjamin offered.

"Oh, here we go. The big moment," Nina said.

The band began a staccato drumroll that rose and fell on the breeze, sometimes sounding like nothing more than a flag snapping in the wind.

"The first runner-up for Weymouth High School homecoming queen is . . ."

"That's it, drag it out, Hardcastle," Nina said.

". . . Zoey Passmore!"

"Hey, she came in second. Cool," Benjamin said. "Any more coffee?"

Nina unscrewed the thermos bottle. "Yeah, if it turns out *Playboy* magazine has nude pictures of K-burger, then Zoey will take over the official duties, whatever they may be."

"Is Jake jumpy or is it just my imagination?" Aisha asked.

"The first runner-up for Weymouth High School homecoming king is . . ."

"Just in case they also have nude photos of Lucas."

". . . Tad Crowley!"

Nina noticed that Claire actually looked disappointed Jake hadn't won the number-two slot. Nina rolled her eyes. Amazing. Claire was acting like it mattered. "Could this be any more bogus? We all know who the winners are; the only suspense was over the runners-up."

"And the new homecoming king is . . ."

The drumroll swelled.

"Lucas Cabral!" Nina yelled out. "But I'm just guessing."

Mr. Hardcastle's face fell as the sound of Nina's

151

shout carried down to the grandstand. But he went ahead as though nothing had happened. "... Lucas Cabral."

"I heard that name somewhere before," Nina said.

Benjamin nudged her in the side. "Together on the next one."

Nina grinned and elbowed Aisha. There was a tittering sound from the people close by. Obviously a number of people had the same idea.

"And the new Weymouth High School homecoming queen is . . ."

"LOUISE KRONENBERGER!" a hundred voices yelled. "BUT WE'RE JUST GUESSING."

Seventeen

After the halftime ceremony was over and Jake was back in his pads and jersey, he went into a toilet stall to do a few more lines. His conscience was now only a whisper in the back of his brain as he tapped the powder out in the crease of a folded piece of pasteboard and used a rolled-up dollar bill as a straw. The initial buzz had begun to wear off and he wanted to hit the field at absolute maximum velocity.

As the team trotted back out to the field he made a race of it, challenging his teammates to catch him and signaling that he was back. Back in a major way.

The very first play was a pass. Fitz had overthrown, as usual, but Jake leapt, got two fingers on the ball, brought it tumbling down, and caught it as he fell for a first down.

A roar went up from the crowd, and an answering roar went through him. This was more like it. He was back in control. He could barely wait for the next play.

In the third quarter the Weymouth team brought the score to within ten points. By the end of the game they were within a point.

They had still lost, but the humiliating first-half had been wiped away. And back in the locker room after the game, the mood was more upbeat than it had been at halftime.

"What the hell," Lars Ehrlich said, "we nearly won and they had linemen big enough to be in the NFL. Did you see that number thirty-two? The guy's a truck."

"This is true," someone else agreed. "Nobody ever expected us to win."

"If you'd played the first half like you played the second half, McRoyan, we *would* have won." Fitz was not ever one to accept a loss gracefully. Normally, neither was Jake. But this was about more than just winning. His own personal honor had been at stake. If he hadn't gotten his act together at the end, the whole school, hell, the whole town, would have pointed to him as the one who blew it. Now at least some self-respect had been salvaged.

Still, Jake was feeling desperately weary, despite the stinging hot shower. More tired than he remembered ever feeling. Too tired to want to go out and celebrate the near-upset with the guys, though a semi-official party had been organized. It was a party for football players and cheerleaders and it would mean rehashing the game half the night.

Only a small amount of the coke was left in his locker, but it ought to be enough to buy him another hour of energy, enough to get to the ferry and home. He went to his locker and slid the vial into the pocket of his jeans.

Then he felt something strange. A circle of silence had formed around him. He looked up guiltily and saw his coach, wearing the grim expression that had silenced the locker room.

"Hey, Coach," he said warily.

"McRoyan, we have a little problem."

154

Jake shrugged. "I know, I blew the first half."

"Yes, you did, but that's not our only problem. The Bangor coach thinks you had an amazing recovery during halftime."

Now the room was dead silent. Jake closed his locker door, a deafening noise.

"Must have been the pep talk you gave us," Jake said.

The coach tilted his head and focused sharply. "The Bangor coach wonders if maybe it wasn't more than a pep talk. He's made a formal request that you be given a drug test."

Jake felt his stomach lurch. He glanced at Lars, but Lars was looking down at the floor. Jake forced a heavy laugh. "He's nuts, Coach. You know I'm not into that stuff."

"Look, Jake," the coach said, kindly for him, "here's the deal: I can't force you to take the test—"

"I have nothing to hide," Jake protested wildly.

"Now, listen to me. Listen to me closely. Are you listening?"

Jake nodded. He could feel the hard knot of the vial in his pocket. His heart was thudding like a sledgehammer in his chest.

"If you agree to take a urine test and it comes up negative, okay. If it comes up positive for any controlled substance, you're off the team permanently. Do you follow me so far?"

"Yes, sir," Jake murmured.

"However, you can refuse to take the test, in which case I will have to suspend you from the team until you agree to take a test. Are you getting this? If you test positive now, you're gone. If you refuse the test, hey, maybe next week you have a change of heart.

155

You take the test, you pass, you're back on the team. Is that clear?''

It was clear. His coach was telling him to refuse. Refuse until the drug was out of his system. But it would mean admitting his guilt. No one would have the slightest doubt as to why he had refused.

"I think drug tests are bull," Fitz said, unexpectedly coming to Jake's defense. "They ought to be unconstitutional."

"The school board doesn't give a rat's ass about the Constitution," the coach said. "This is *their* policy, although personally I'll tell you right now any athlete who thinks he's going to improve his performance over the long run with drugs is just a fool. Make your choice, McRoyan."

Jake raised his head and tried to look his coach in the eye. But he found himself staring off over the heads of everyone around him. His face burned. His hands felt clammy. His pulse was racing, though whether it was from anxiety or the lingering effects of the cocaine, he couldn't tell.

"I don't think I'll take the test, Coach."

The coach nodded grimly. "I kind of thought that might be your decision. You're suspended for a week. If you can pass a test then, I'll put you back on the team."

"Yes, sir," Jake said.

"Everyone gets one free mistake in my book. But don't pull this again, McRoyan. Whatever the damned school board policy, *my* policy is I don't have druggies on my team."

Jake left the gym with the burning feeling of eyes following him. He dodged around the moving mass of people heading out toward the parking lot, some in

156

high spirits, others rehashing the game, parents trying to be cool with their kids, and their kids wishing the parents would just go home so they could take off to the dozen or more parties already under way.

One or two yells followed him, derisive remarks from some, a more encouraging cry from someone else, but he didn't acknowledge anyone. He pushed on through, trying to get as far away from them all as quickly as he could.

He had lost the game. That was the fact. And he had been suspended for suspicion of drug use. If he didn't clear the next drug test, this would go on his permanent record, and no college, not even the humble Maine schools he'd applied to as safeties, would be interested in a known druggie athlete.

He fished in his pocket for the vial of cocaine and blindly threw it into the bushes.

He ran toward the dock, realizing even as he ran that he had no good choices. His parents would probably take the water taxi back to the island. His friends—and Claire—would all be on the ferry. He couldn't avoid them all.

He needed time to think. He needed to disappear somewhere for a while, wait for the water taxi's last run, after his parents were safely gone.

Suddenly, down the street, came a loud group of kids, a mix of seniors and juniors. Some he knew fairly well, like Tad Crowley. Others he knew only by sight.

"Hey, yo, big Jake!" Tad yelled. "What's up, man?"

Jake shrugged. "Not much."

"You want to party? My mom's out with her boyfriend and we have . . . *obtained* . . . a keg."

Tad was obviously pretty well lit already, Jake

realized. They weren't exactly in the same circle, and if Tad weren't feeling unnaturally expansive, he never would have invited Jake over. Still, it was a place to hang for a while. And a couple of brews would take the edge off.

Tad Crowley's home was an apartment in an old, four-story brick building right in the quaint Portside section of Weymouth. Jake was able to lean out of the window and see the ferry landing. Perfect. Easy, downhill walking distance to the water taxi.

Inside, the lights were low and the stereo was cranked up on some old Grateful Dead. Jake found the keg resting in the kitchen sink on a pile of slushy ice. Louise Kronenberger was bent at the waist, her lips wrapped around the tap, swallowing while a handful of other people stood around counting, "Fifteen, sixteen, seventeen . . ."

At twenty Louise broke away and came up for air, gasping and giggling and looking flushed. Tad Crowley started to take her place, but then he noticed Jake. "Hey, your turn, man; you've got to need it more than me, running around all night and all."

Jake squatted and took the tap in his mouth. He pressed the lever and the cool beer began to flow while the crowd began a count. At twenty-nine he came up for air, feeling bleary and giddy.

That was better. Much better. He sat down heavily on a couch and sighed in relief. This music wasn't his favorite kind of stuff usually, but it sounded cool right now. Laid back, and that's what he needed. He needed to relax.

He began rubbing at a sore spot on his thigh where one of the Bangor linemen had nailed him hard with his helmet.

"You hurt yourself?" Louise sat beside him. Close

158

beside him. She was wearing a skirt that rode up as she squirmed to make herself comfortable.

"Just a bruise," Jake said. The thick sound of his voice was funny. He smiled broadly.

"Caught a buzz yet?"

"Either that or my mouth just stopped working," he said.

"We wouldn't want that," Louise said. "So. Jake McRoyan partying with all us lowlifes. Aren't the Virgin Islanders having a private party tonight?" She laughed appreciatively at her own joke.

Jake stared at her legs. When she moved, he could see a flash of her white panties.

"I'm thirsty again," he said.

"Me too. What a coincidence."

"Too bad I can't walk," he joked.

Louise stood up. She swayed as she reached for his hand and pretended to be hauling him to his feet.

"Uh-oh, Louise found herself some new meat," a laughing voice said from somewhere.

Jake stood up, spread his arms to gain his balance, and followed Louise to the kitchen.

"What did I do last time?" Louise wondered, wrinkling her brow with concentration. "Twenty. This time, twenty-one. You count, okay?"

Jake kept count as well as he could, but he repeated fifteen twice, which brought Louise up sputtering in hysterics. "You're lucky you have a really, really great body," she said. " 'Cause you can't count worth a damn."

Jake bent to the tap. This time neither of them kept count. Jake drank till his lungs burned from lack of air. When he stood up, the world was reeling.

"Now . . .'m buzz," he said. " 'S go siddown."

He took a wobbly step back toward the living room,

but somehow he didn't reach the couch. Instead, he realized, he'd come to be lying on his back on an unmade bed. Louise was beside him. She was undoing the buttons on his shirt, her fingers fumbling.

" 'ts goin' on?" he asked.

Louise didn't answer. She finished opening his shirt and began running her hands and lips over his chest. Her fingers felt like ice, but her mouth was hot on his.

Jake squinted, trying to focus. The coke had worn off completely, leaving a weariness that had been deepened by the beer. He felt barely awake, in some halfway state between consciousness and nothingness. "Claire?" he asked.

"Yeah, it's Claire," a girl's voice said, laughing.

Jake nodded, closing his eyes. "Love you."

Eighteen

"It's kind of eerie being out this late, or early, or whatever it is," Nina said. "I'll bet the four of us are the only people awake on this entire island."

"Actually, I think *you're* the only one really awake," Aisha grumbled.

"That's because I'm a creature of the night," Nina said. Aisha pulled the car into a U-turn to pull away from the front of Nina's house and head toward the dock. A light rain was falling, making the streets glisten and blanking out what little moonlight filtered down through the clouds. Zoey was breathing heavily in the backseat. Not exactly snoring, but the stage just before snoring. She was lying against Lucas, who had never been entirely awake to begin with. "You got a stereo, Aisha? I think we're losing Dan and Roseanne back there."

Aisha pointed at the dashboard. "It gets only one station. Country."

"Pass," Nina said.

Zoey woke up with a snort. "I'm awake, I'm awake."

"We know you are," Aisha said, grinning at Nina.

Zoey rubbed her eyes. "I do hope Christopher gets

161

better soon. I don't know how he does this every night. He's like the Energizer Bunny.''

"Was Benjamin awake when you left?" Nina asked Zoey.

"Are you going to be like this?" Zoey asked grumpily. "I mean, if you and Benjamin are going to be seeing each other, then you have to leave me out of it."

"I was just curious," Nina said with a nonchalant shrug. She dug out a cigarette and popped it into the corner of her mouth.

"You know, if you're going to *not* smoke something, Nina, why don't you *not* smoke cigars?" Aisha suggested. "Then you could look really weird."

Nina puffed contentedly.

"So. Not that I'm getting into this," Zoey began, "but how did everything seem with Benjamin tonight?"

"Not that you're getting into it, it was no biggie. I mean, it was like all of us together doing something. We've all done stuff together lots of times."

"I guess tomorrow night's the big test, huh?" Aisha said. "Dancing, holding hands, screaming little bits of conversation at each other over the music." She wiggled her eyebrows meaningfully. "The big *K*.''

Nina sat up. "The big kitty? The big kelp? The big karma?"

Aisha tucked her thumb into her fist, making a little mouth, and kissed it noisily.

"I'm not thinking about that," Nina said. "I'm only going to deal with things as they come up. Scratch that," she added hastily as Aisha and Zoey began to giggle. "You guys know what I mean."

"Are we there yet?" Lucas asked, coming out of his stupor.

"You know, I could do this myself," Aisha said. "If you guys are going to bitch the whole time."

"Island solidarity," Lucas muttered.

The car pulled into the brightly lit zone of the ferry landing. The plastic-wrapped newspapers lay waiting. Nearby lay a large bundle of rags. Nina wondered why anyone would pile a bunch of rags on the dock, but then her eye was drawn by a slight movement.

"Hey, hey!" she cried. "That's a person."

Aisha braked and the four of them piled out, approaching the inanimate figure cautiously.

"It's Jake," Zoey said, putting her hand over her heart. She knelt beside him and tried to wake him by grabbing his hand. "He's ice-cold."

"He must have hopped the water taxi when it came to drop off the papers," Lucas said. "I'm guessing Jake may have been having a little too much fun." He nudged him fairly hard in the side with his boot. "Come on, Jake. Party's over."

Jake stirred and blinked. He squinted to focus. "Wha—?"

"You're on the dock," Zoey said.

"And he's in deep flop if he shows up back at his house and his dad sees him like this," Nina said. "I can't believe *Joke* is this messed up. Just because we lost the dumb game?"

"It's not about the game," Zoey said. "Come on, Jake, we have to get you out of here."

"Zoey?" he said thickly.

"Yes, Jake. Come on. Try and stand up. Lucas, give me a hand."

Lucas looked doubtful, but came and took one of Jake's arms, draped it over his shoulders, and tried to

163

get him up. Jake lay limp at first, but finally staggered up. He wobbled for a moment, then stumbled to the dock railing. He leaned over and began vomiting into the water below.

Zoey went over and stroked his head, murmuring soft encouragements.

Lucas wasn't amused. "Should we just leave him here to sleep it off?"

Jake finished and stepped back from the railing. Zoey used her scarf to wipe his mouth.

"What are you all looking at?" Jake demanded belligerently.

"Jake, no one is looking at you," Zoey insisted.

"Leave me alone, you . . ." He searched for the right word. "All of you," he finished with a bearlike sweep of his arms.

Nina realized that Zoey was crying silently, biting her thumb.

"Let's take him to my house," Nina said suddenly, surprising herself. "My dad sleeps like a corpse. We can stash him in our guest room."

"I don't know how your sister would feel about that," Aisha said.

"He's sort of her boyfriend," Nina said. "Used to be sort of her boyfriend. Whatever."

"Good idea," Lucas agreed quickly. He looked pointedly at Zoey. "He's *Claire's* boyfriend."

"Come on, Jake, get in the car," Zoey said. She took his arm, a frail figure beside him, and led him away.

"Look, Lucas," Nina told him in a low voice, "it doesn't mean anything."

"Really," Aisha agreed. "They *were* together for a long time. You can't expect her not to try and help him out when he's this screwed up."

164

"You're the only one, Zo," Jake said as Zoey tried to push him into the backseat. "Everyone else . . . Screw 'em."

"Watch your head. That's right. Easy."

"Don't take me home, okay? Wade . . . he'll laugh 'cause I . . .'cause I think . . ."

Nina felt a chill. She saw the hard expression on Lucas's face soften a little and he turned to her.

"Sort of the downside of true love, huh, Nina?" he said. "You still sure you want to start playing this game?"

Claire woke to the sound of car doors closing. There was no nocturnal traffic on Chatham Island normally, and she was sleeping with her windows open, just her head sticking out from under the goose-down comforter.

She wrapped the comforter around herself and went to her window. In the front yard Lucas and Zoey were manhandling a big, shambling figure between them. Nina and Aisha ran ahead to open the front door. Claire glanced at her clock. It was almost four in the morning.

She heard the sound of heavy steps on the stairs and loud whispers. Claire waited. Finally, after ten minutes, there was the sound of footsteps retreating. The car drove off.

Claire dropped the comforter back on her bed and put on warm sweats and a bathrobe. She went down to the lower floor, retrieved several items from the bathroom she shared with Nina, and found Jake snoring in the rear guest bedroom.

They had pulled covers on over his clothes, stuffed a pillow under his head, taken off his shoes, and closed the blinds so that he would sleep through the dawn.

Claire set vitamin pills, aspirin, and a pitcher of tap water on the nightstand. Then she sat on the bed beside him and lifted his head. "Come on, Jake, just wake up for two seconds."

His eyes opened without focusing. "Thirsty," he croaked.

"Yeah, I thought you might be." It had been a long time since she'd been drunk, but she remembered what it felt like. She put the pitcher of water to his lips and he drank greedily. Then she poured three vitamin B pills and two aspirins into her palm. "Open up."

She tossed the pills in his mouth and gave him the pitcher again. "That will help. A little, anyway. If you need to throw up, use this wastebasket. All you have to do is roll over."

"Claire?"

"Yes, Jake."

"Claire?"

"Yes, Jake, it's me."

". . . kicked me off the team."

Claire bit her lip. He'd been kicked off the team? Was that real, or some drunken hallucination? "Don't think about it now. Just lie back and close your eyes." She pressed him back against the pillows.

In a moment he was unconscious again. Claire sat in the small rocking chair at the foot of the bed and closed her eyes.

"I don't seem to have a very good effect on the guys I hook up with, do I?" she asked the darkness. "First Lucas. He ended up spending two years in Youth Authority. And now Jake."

"What am I supposed to do about you?" she whispered. "I can't change what happened. I can't bring Wade back to life."

If Jake were a different person, he would be able to get past this loyalty to his brother. While Wade was alive, he had relentlessly belittled and harassed Jake, making him the object of every joke, feeding his own ego at the expense of his adoring little brother. And now, it was as if even in death, Wade was finding a way to make Jake miserable.

But Jake wasn't interested in the truth about Wade. Wade was his big brother, period. He would probably never allow himself to see any further than that. And Claire, whatever else she might be, was the person responsible, in Jake's mind, for Wade's death.

In the same position, *she* would find a way to resolve the conflict. She was not a person who believed in absolutes, and she refused to be trapped by them.

But Jake was a different person. There were no shades of gray for Jake: it was all black and white, right and wrong. To love her was to betray Wade. She could not coexist in his mind alongside the memory of Wade, and the more Jake tried, the more he destroyed himself.

Claire sighed. Wade could not be made to go away. Which meant that in the end there was only one solution.

She felt something crawling down her cheek and touched it with her finger. She was surprised to discover that it was a tear.

Zoey led Lucas up the dark stairs to her room. Lucas's father was up and on his way to work each day before dawn, like all the professional fishermen and lobstermen on the island. Lucas didn't want to run into him and face the possibility of having to explain why he was out.

Zoey closed the door behind them and flipped on the light. It had seemed like a perfectly normal thing, to invite Lucas to sleep over for a few hours. But now, with him in her bedroom, both moving quietly like a pair of burglars, it began to seem a little more dubious.

Lucas yawned. "I'm beat. What a bizarre night. Dragging Jake up the stairs, driving around like vampires on the prowl throwing papers." He sat down on Zoey's bed and unlaced his boots.

Zoey fidgeted nervously, not quite sure how to proceed. Normally, she would change into her favorite Boston Bruins jersey and crawl under the covers.

"Um, I'll hit the bathroom," she said, snatching up her nightshirt. She brushed her teeth and combed her hair and changed into the thin cotton shirt. It came most of the way down to her knees, so it wasn't exactly provocative. Still, it was what she *slept* in. Not what she wore when she had guests over.

She went back to the room and found the lights turned off, for which she was grateful. Maybe Lucas had already fallen asleep. That would be best.

She slid beneath the covers and had the shocking and completely unfamiliar experience of touching a bare leg with her foot. She nearly yelped out loud. But that was being silly. They were practically adults. It wasn't like they couldn't sleep in the same location without it being some big thing. Zoey repeated the phrase in her mind—yes, that's all it was, sleeping in the same location.

She rolled onto her side, facing away from him. "Good night," she whispered.

"Don't I get a good-night kiss?"

"Sure." She twisted her head toward him, intending to accept a light peck on the lips. Instead his arm went around her and he drew her against him. His kiss left her gasping.

"Lucas," she said.

"Yes?"

"We are *not* doing that."

Long silence. His face was inches away in the darkness. His arms were around her. She could hear his breath coming fast.

"Um . . . Why not?"

Zoey shrugged, feeling uncertain. "I just haven't decided that's something I want to do. At least not yet."

"How about if I've decided that it's something I *do* want to do?"

"It's one of those things that kind of has to be unanimous," Zoey said. "Come on, you know I only let you come up here because of your dad. You know I wasn't planning on having sex."

"No?"

"No."

"Okay. Excuse me for just a minute," Lucas said with deliberate politeness. He rolled away and in the darkness Zoey could hear him screaming into his pillow in frustration. It went on for longer than she would have expected. Finally he surfaced again.

"Did that help?" Zoey asked tentatively.

"No. It didn't. Look, Zoey, I don't know how it is for girls, but for guys this whole thing is sort of important. In the way that air is sort of important if you want to breathe."

"Well, it is with girls, too, but—"

"See? That's the problem. With girls there's a *but*. With guys there's no *but* anything. It's like, if some-

169

one said to me right now, you can have sex with Zoey, but we have to cut off your hand, I'd probably say, okay, what the hell, a hook will look cool.''

''That's kind of flattering in a way,'' Zoey said, trying to defuse the level of tension. ''Insane, but flattering.''

''Insane, exactly. That's what it makes me, insane.''

Zoey sat up in the bed, drawing her knees up and encircling them with her arms. ''Lucas, look, I think I understand how you feel, but it *has* to be different for girls. First of all, guys don't get pregnant, have kids, and end up on welfare. Second of all, girls have a greater risk of getting AIDS and all the other popular sexually transmitted diseases. And third, the problem with you guys is that sex is *all* you think about, whereas females, being a little higher on the evolutionary scale, also think about things like commitment and love and all.''

''But I do love you,'' Lucas said, sounding almost desperate.

''Let me ask you a question. Do you even have a condom with you?''

''A condom? Do I have one?''

''I thought so. See, you love me, but you're willing to take the risk I could get pregnant or catch something.''

''So, you're saying if I get some condoms . . . ?''

''No, I'm saying when *I* decide *I'm* ready, you'll be the very first person to know.''

Lucas lay silent in the dark. Whether he was seething in anger or nodding in agreement, she couldn't be sure.

''I'll be the first person to know,'' he repeated. ''Not Jake?''

Zoey sighed. "Lucas, I was just trying to help him out because he was in bad shape. Would you like me if I were the kind of person who just walked away?"

"I think I'm going to have to scream into my pillow some more."

"You're not the only one," Zoey said softly. "You know, I do love you, too."

"Yeah, right."

"Go to sleep."

"Hmm. Can I tell everyone we slept together? I mean, we are, technically."

"Go to sleep."

"Good-night kiss?"

"Sleep."

She heard him scream into his pillow once more, and a few minutes later they were both asleep.

Love is a fairly useless word. It is imprecise. It isn't specific.

You love your mom, you love your country, you love ice cream, you love the girl you love. I love you like a brother, I love the smell of napalm in the morning, you're gonna love this one, I ~~olve~~ love what you do for me Toyota, gotta love it. Same word, different meanings.

Even romantic love has all sorts of different levels. I mean, Romeo had a different thing going with Juliet than Mr. and Mrs. Macbeth had together. Although, who knows? Maybe if Romeo ~~smf~~ and Juliet had survived, gotten married, grown old, they too might have ended up murdering their house-guests and chatting with witches.

My point is, there are four women who are important in my life. My mom, whom I love. Your basic filial love. My sister, Zoey, whom I also love. This would be your brotherly love.

Then there's Claire, whom I love. Romantic love. The boy-girl thing, with sort of a self-destructive, why-am-I-doing-this? sort of edge mixed in. Love as a form of protracted conflict.

Then there's Nina. I love Nina in kind of the same way I love Zoey. Like a sister. Except she's not my sister, which means that all the while I've ~~beeeen~~ been aware that possibilities existed beyond the very definite limitations of brotherly love. Aware of the possibilities, but determined not to think about them and screw up a really good friendship.

And there's something a little disturbing about the idea of a person migrating from the "love-you-like-a-sister" category over into the much more intense "can't-wait-to-kiss-you-again" category. It's no different than one day saying, "Man, I love ice cream" and the next day saying, "No, I mean I really love ice cream. I want to have Ben and Jerry's baby."

It still seems like something that ought to be illegal, or at least frowned upon.

Nineteen

They caught the seven-forty ferry from the island and rode across choppy seas, under a high, full moon, toward the glittering mainland and, Nina thought melodramatically, *destiny*.

"You look . . ." Benjamin said, letting the question hang.

"Fetching," Nina supplied. "It's complimentary, but not over the top."

Benjamin smiled. "And I particularly like that . . . um, that—"

"Dress."

"And the color, why it's . . . it's . . ."

"Depressing," Nina said. "It's black."

"Still, it goes nicely with your eyes—"

"Which are gray."

"Yes, I know that," Benjamin said smoothly. "I was asking how many. Two, right?"

"Arranged so that there's one on either side of my nose," Nina said. "I read in *YM* that's the fashionable arrangement for eyes this season."

"And me? How do I look?" he asked, giving a little turn on the steel deck.

As usual, he looked good, having a wardrobe that consisted almost entirely of subtle, muted colors that worked well in almost any combination. "Well, I don't want to make you self-conscious," Nina said, "but the green plaid doesn't really go all that well with the yellow stripes. Or the paisley."

"Damn. I've made another fashion faux pas. Imagine my embarrassment."

They both laughed and Nina realized she was feeling almost relaxed, as if this night didn't represent a major change in her life. As if there weren't a dozen horrible scenarios floating around in the back of her mind, ranging from slightly embarrassing to move-to-another-state embarrassing.

Benjamin fell quiet for a moment and Nina didn't interrupt. He was listening to the sound of the engines, the intermittent crash of waves against the hull, and the murmur of other conversations. She listened with him, and searched his familiar face for a sign that he had magically changed in the way he felt about her. Was he being nicer? Gentler? More considerate? Probably not, she concluded. Benjamin was just being himself, neither more, nor less.

"I like the way you do that," he said.

"Do what?"

"The way you know when I want to listen, and you wait very patiently."

"Sure," Nina said, feeling awkward. She began looking in her purse for her cigarettes.

"So. Aren't we all supposed to be surprised that Claire and Jake are going to this dance together?"

Claire. Nina had wondered how long they'd be able to go without her name coming up. She looked across the deck and spotted them, Jake and Claire, leaning back together by the stern railing, close but not touching. And not really talking very much, either. "I think Jake owed her big time for last night," Nina said.

"And I guess she really wanted to go to this dance."

"She does have a way of getting what she wants," Benjamin observed.

"That's what you like about her, isn't it?" Nina asked.

Benjamin smiled and gave the uncanny impression that he was looking at her from behind his sunglasses, trying to read her expression. "How about if we make a deal right up front here. How about if we don't talk about Claire?"

"What'll we talk about instead?"

"Hmmm. Infomercials. Favorite cheeses. What to bring to a desert island. And the meaning of life."

"Okay. Sounds cool. But we'd better start with the easy one first."

"Meaning of life," Benjamin said, nodding.

"Let's have it down by the time we dock."

The ferry came into Weymouth and the seven of them disembarked, part of a sparse crowd. It was difficult for islanders to do much nighttime partying on the mainland, since the last ferry returning to the islands left at nine. Late-night functions like dances meant taking the more expensive water taxi home.

Aisha felt a little strange, walking through the streets with her friends. Tonight she was the only one not part of a couple. Even Nina had a date, and she and Benjamin were talking away, occasionally laughing out loud. It was nice to see Nina having a good time that involved a member of the opposite sex, but it did drive home to Aisha the fact that she was the odd person in a group of seven.

Although, come to think of it, she felt happier than Claire and Jake looked.

Official visiting hours at the hospital were over, but

the feeling had been that they should give it a try just the same. The truth was, if they hadn't planned to go and see Christopher, Aisha would have just stayed home.

Aisha had discovered a door on an earlier visit that bypassed the heavily monitored emergency room, and she led them inside. The brightly lit hospital corridors were mostly empty, and they made their way quickly, suppressing giggles and making morbid jokes, like a group of party crashers with very bad taste in parties.

Aisha knocked at the door to Christopher's room and, on hearing a muffled response, they went in. She was relieved to see that Christopher was sitting up, looking relatively normal again. The swelling had gone down sufficiently to allow him to see out of both eyes. He was flipping through the channels on the TV.

"Hey, what is this?" he asked. "You didn't all have to play dress-up just to come visit me."

Aisha gave him a little kiss. "We're on our way to the homecoming dance."

Christopher cocked an eyebrow suspiciously. "And who's your date?"

"We're all sharing," Zoey piped up. "Actually, I'm sharing Lucas two ways, with Louise Kronenberger and with Aisha." She sent Lucas an exaggeratedly suspicious look.

"Still on the good painkillers?" Lucas asked.

"No, and I've noticed something—TV is much better when you're delirious. Thank God I'm getting out tomorrow. I'd lose my mind if I had to spend any more time in here. I even lost my roommate." He indicated the vacant bed across the room.

"Lost?" Nina asked.

"Not as in dead," Christopher said. "As in gone home."

"Tomorrow we'll have you all set up," Aisha promised. "The Governor's Room. Jacuzzi, big four-poster bed, antiques, and my mom, who wants to try out a bunch of recipes on a helpless guinea pig."

"I get to move in next," Jake said, speaking for the first time.

"Yeah, well, you guys have all been very cool," Christopher said, suddenly serious. "Delivering my papers and all. Zoey's dad covering for me at the restaurant. Mr. Geiger I know has covered most of my bill here in the hospital."

"Liberal white guilt," Nina said with a shrug. "Besides, the old man's rich."

"Of course he did say he wants the papers up on the front porch from now on," Claire said. "Not halfway across the yard."

Christopher smiled crookedly. "I'm just saying everyone's been very cool in this. Especially certain people." He put his arm around Aisha's waist.

"Island solidarity," Benjamin said. "When we're not busy stabbing each other in the back, we try and help each other out."

"Hey, you guys better get going," Christopher said. "I know Lucas has vital duties as homecoming king."

"Please don't use that phrase," Lucas pleaded. "Whenever I hear it, I get a headache."

"Go on, before the nurse busts you all," Christopher said. He took Aisha's face in his hands and gave her a kiss on the lips. "That's the best I can do until these stitches come out," he apologized.

"That was plenty good," Aisha said with feeling. The others had started to leave discreetly. "We'll have to work together on the period of rehabilitation."

"I'll see you, babe."

178

She kissed him on the head and opened the door to the hallway. The others were bunched together, making *aww, wasn't that sweet* faces.

"Hey, Lucas," Christopher called out. "Can you come here a minute?"

Lucas looked surprised. He went back into the room.

Lucas was inside for several minutes. When he came out, he looked distracted and grim. But he quickly plastered on a smile. "Come on, let's get out of this place."

"What was that all about?" Zoey asked.

Lucas shrugged. "Oh, he just, uh . . . he said he wanted me to, you know, keep an eye out for Aisha. Manly protective stuff."

Aisha laughed as though she believed him, but she could see that Zoey's eyes were clouded with doubt. And Lucas sounded less than convincing.

But an orderly turned down the hallway, forcing them into a panicky, giggling race for the exit, and the moment for voicing suspicions was past.

Twenty

The multipurpose room was a sea of bodies in motion, bouncing, spinning, hair tossing, arms and legs that seemed to belong to more than one body. The lights were low and filtered through pink and red crepe paper, deepening shadows and making bare skin glow unnaturally, as though everyone in the room had just come from a tanning bed.

The band onstage was one everyone had seen before, and most had danced to before. They played an eclectic mix, one minute hard rocking, then veering off into sanitized, school-board-approved rap.

"So," Nina said, surveying the scene. "This is a school dance."

"Haven't you been to one or two dances?" Benjamin asked her, speaking loudly over the music.

"Maybe for a total of ten minutes," Nina said. "Hey. Where are you guys going?"

All the island contingent had arrived together, but Claire and Jake had already wandered off in one direction, and now Zoey and Lucas and Aisha were sidling away.

"Lucas has to go find out when the big presentation is!" Zoey yelled in her ear. "Eesh and I are just going to hit the girls' room."

180

"Wait, I'll go with you," Nina said, leaving Benjamin's side.

Zoey shook her head. "Nina, stop worrying; you'll be fine. Don't think of it as a date. You're just hanging out with Benjamin."

"There's a band and I'm wearing a dress," Nina protested. "That's not hanging out."

"Bye, Nina," Zoey said with a wink.

Nina watched her disappear and then went back to Benjamin. One or two kids on the dance floor were sending looks in their direction. But it had not been the full stop-and-stare she'd feared.

"How's it look?" Benjamin asked.

"Like teen night in hell," Nina said bleakly.

"Cool," Benjamin said with a smile.

"People are looking at me."

"Admiringly?"

"No, more like *What's the deal? Why is Nina here? She never comes to dances.*"

"Since when do you care if people look at you?"

"Since I know what they're wondering is, Does she have a date? Benjamin? No way, Benjamin wouldn't go out with Nina. Besides, she doesn't even like guys, does she?" Nina was beginning to feel the first trickle of panic. People were staring, more and more now. Each of them analyzing the situation. Each of them remembering what they'd heard about Nina's uncle. Hundreds of amateur psychiatrists working up their analysis of her while they danced and rubbed their bodies together.

Nina swallowed hard. She felt something touch her arm, then slide down to her hand. Benjamin's fingers wrapped around the fist Nina had formed.

"Come on, Nina," Benjamin said. "This is the moment when you either go forward or back."

"I know what they're all thinking."

"Ten minutes from now they'll have forgotten all about you."

"It's like I'm trying to be someone else. That's always a mistake. Be yourself, right? And I'm trying to be some other person."

"No, it's like you're trying to be yourself without a lot of old fear getting in the way, Nina. Hey. Did you bring your shades?"

For a moment Nina was confused. Shades? Then she remembered. With her free hand she opened her purse and looked inside. "Uh-huh."

"So?"

Nina hesitated. Her stomach felt like it was turning. She was sure she must be blushing brightly; she could feel the heat in her face. And she was definitely avoiding eye contact with everyone. She could walk away now, go back and catch the ferry home. Benjamin would find someone to spend the rest of the evening with.

She would be alone and safe. She could remain the same person she'd always been, not have to break new ground and suddenly try to emerge from the years of shame and secrets.

There was a sudden break in the music. With a loud twang the lead guitarist had broken a string. Relative quiet descended as the music faded out.

"I'm guessing we have everyone's attention now," Benjamin said dryly.

It was true. Without the distraction of the music there wasn't much for people to do but stare, subtly or openly, at what seemed like the impossible spectacle of Nina Geiger and Benjamin Passmore holding hands.

Nina took a deep breath. "Okay," she muttered

under her breath, "now that I have everyone's attention." She reached into her bag and pulled out a Lucky Strike and stuck it in the corner of her mouth. Her hands were shaking so badly she almost couldn't do it. Then she retrieved the sunglasses, the Ray Bans identical to the ones Benjamin wore, snapped them open, and put them on.

Finally, with a supreme effort, she unclenched her fist. Her fingers, clammy and sweaty, intertwined with Benjamin's.

The music started up again. The crowd started dancing.

"Are we still being stared at?" Benjamin asked.

"A little less," Nina admitted. Her teeth were chattering as if she were cold.

"Well, we are officially on a date then, I guess."

"So, I guess we'd better dance," Nina said, trying not to sound like she was telling the dentist to go ahead and drill.

Benjamin laughed. "You think it's been scary so far. Wait till you're around me when I'm dancing."

Lucas danced a little with Zoey, and danced once or twice with Aisha, and drank some punch. But it was hard to get into the party atmosphere. Christopher had pretty well killed any remaining chance that he might enjoy this evening.

Christopher had called him back into his hospital room to ask whether Lucas could get him a gun.

A *gun*. Like Lucas was a gangster or something. He'd told Christopher to forget it. First of all, he'd been busted for drunk driving leading to a fatality, not for holding up 7-Elevens. Second of all, he hadn't even been guilty of the drunk driving.

Third of all, getting a gun so he could go looking

for the guys who beat him up was dangerous and stupid beyond imagination.

But Christopher had sounded determined. It was a matter of getting his respect back, he said. Most of the serious screwups Lucas had known in YA were there over one type of respect or another. Respect was a popular word among violent losers. He'd told Christopher that, but Christopher wasn't thinking clearly.

Lucas wondered how good his reasoning would be under similar circumstances. Probably about the same as Christopher's, he had to admit.

It was going to force a grim choice on him. He could either stand back while Christopher tried to handle things on his own. Or he could drop the dime on Snake, and maybe have to face the consequences.

After a while one of the girls from the homecoming committee came and found him. Perfect. He was really in the mood for some more b.s.

"I have to go get ready for this dumb-ass ceremony dance thing," Lucas told Zoey, leaning to put his lips to her ear.

"Good luck," Zoey said. "Aisha and I will spend the time picking up guys."

Lucas gave her a dirty look and Zoey grinned back angelically.

He went back to the room behind the bandstand, where the music was reduced by cinder-block walls to a dull, throbbing noise like a bad headache. Half a dozen girls and guys from the organizing committee, the principal, and two teacher-chaperons were there, milling around importantly, along with Louise Kronenberger, looking flushed and happy.

She tossed her voluminous brown mane and looked him slowly up and down. "Finally, our big moment," she said.

"Yeah," Lucas said unenthusiastically.

"They already explained to me, we wait till Hardcastle's given his speech and put everyone to sleep. Then the band starts up, slow dance, out we go, take a little bow, and dance around the floor."

"I can't slow dance worth a damn," Lucas said.

"I tried to tell you we should practice."

"Zoey wouldn't have been real happy about that idea."

"Zoey," Louise said impishly, as if the name were a joke. "Zoey doesn't have to worry about *you*, does she?"

"No, she doesn't," Lucas said.

"I know, I know. My reputation precedes me. But really, Lucas, at least ten percent of my reputation is exaggerated." She laughed gaily at the joke. "Seriously, just hold on to me and I'll get you through it." She gave him a look from beneath half-closed lids.

There was a flurry of activity as Mr. Hardcastle and the student who was to introduce him left the room, followed by the two teachers and the rest of the committee members.

They were alone. Louise moved closer, smiling at the way he sidled away. "Like my dress?" she asked.

"What there is of it," Lucas said, keeping his eyes firmly on her face and away from the cleavage on display.

"Boy, Zoey does have you whipped," Louise said.

"We island kids have very low libidos," Lucas joked, still backing away. "Toxic ferry fumes or something."

"I wouldn't say that," Louise said dryly. "Jake's an islander."

Lucas knew instinctively that he did not, under any circumstances, want to ask Louise what she was talk-

185

ing about. Unfortunately, that didn't stop her.

"Yeah, we had a very nice little party last night," she said, laughing all the while. "Although I have to admit, I think he may have thought I was someone else."

Lucas sighed. Perfect. What was it with people that they were constantly dumping their secrets on him? Zoey had already given him hell for knowing that Christopher was being unfaithful to Aisha. Then there had been Christopher's brilliant gun idea.

Now K-burger had just announced that she had seduced Jake. Wonderful. Who was he going to piss off by keeping *this* secret? He knew who he'd piss off by telling.

"Look, I didn't hear that, okay?" Lucas said.

Louise shrugged. "I'm sorry, I like guys. And guys like me. Usually, at least, when they don't have some girl's leash around their . . . necks."

"I love Zoey," Lucas said, feeling virtuous. It was a damned shame Zoey wasn't there to witness his stellar performance.

"Yeah, but Zoey's hanging on to the big *V*, isn't she? I don't know why. I mean, Lucas, you could have any girl in this school. Zoey ought to realize that."

"It's none of your business," Lucas said coldly.

Louise laughed. "In other words, I'm right about Zoey."

The door to the room opened and one of the committee girls said, "Okay, it's time. As soon as you hear the applause die down after Mr. Hardcastle gets done speaking."

"That shouldn't take long," Lucas said.

"I can't believe you're enough of a wimp to let Zoey control you, Lucas. I had this image of you as

186

being more . . . I don't know. Tougher. I thought you were something special.''

"Let's just get this over with," Lucas said. Louise wasn't the first person tonight to have a confused image of him.

"Okay. But while we're dancing close, and you have your arms around me, keep in mind that there are girls in the world beside Zoey the Pure.''

Twenty-one

"I guess this is the big moment," Nina said. She was standing by the refreshments table with Benjamin. They were still warm and flushed from dancing, though the lengthy speech by Mr. Hardcastle, having something vaguely to do with why Weymouth High was such a truly swell school, had given them a chance to cool off a little.

"Spotlight up," Nina announced. "And here's our happy couple."

"'Symbols of all that's right with Weymouth High,'" Benjamin quoted sardonically from the principal's speech. "Aren't you glad you came? You'd have missed all this magnificence."

"I am glad I came," Nina said. She looked at him, and reminded herself for the hundredth time that he was her date. Her actual date. And better than that, he was a guy she liked more than she'd thought possible. "I'm very glad."

"You're not going all sincere on me, are you?"

Nina smiled. "I would never do that to you, Benjamin." The band began to play, a slow, almost mournful tune. "Oh, this is nice. Lucas is trying to hold her at arm's length, and Louise is trying to squeeze her big buffers right up into his face."

"Gee, if I'd known that, *I* would have tried to be homecoming king," Benjamin said.

Nina punched him in the arm, and he groaned. It was a proprietary action, Nina realized, like she was jealous that he would think about another girl, but it had happened naturally, without her even thinking about it. And Benjamin had acted like it was perfectly normal.

"You know, I *never* look at other girls," Benjamin said self-mockingly.

"Now I'm definitely glad I came. Zoey is standing a few feet away from them, doing this smile she does when she's really on slow boil."

Zoey was standing with Aisha, watching Lucas move Louise around the floor with the minute attention of a cat watching a mouse.

"Should have been you," Aisha said comfortingly. "Homecoming queen, I mean."

"That's not what I care about," Zoey said. "Although it would be nice to win something, *some*time. It's just why couldn't it have been Amelia or Kay or Marie who won?"

"Or for that matter, it could have been Jake or Tad or someone else who won for king."

"That would have been okay, too," Zoey agreed.

"Basically, anyone but the combination of Lucas and Louise," Aisha said.

"Basically."

"You shouldn't be worried just because she has bigger boobs than you do, Zoey. You put way too much on that. That's really *not* all that guys think about. Besides, you know Lucas loves you."

"It's not her boobs I'm worried about," Zoey said. "Give me some credit. It's just that, well . . . you

189

know what everyone says about Louise."

"You mean 'Lay Down Louise'? 'Easy Louisie'? I may have heard certain ugly rumors," Aisha said.

Zoey shrugged and looked away in embarrassment. "Lucas has sort of been wanting to, you know ... And I've been saying no. Or at least, not yet."

"Look, Zoey, you can't get into just competing—"

Her words were cut off as the song ended and the audience applauded more or less enthusiastically for the end of the big ceremonial dance.

Lucas smiled grimly and nearly pushed Louise away. Zoey found that extremely gratifying.

"I guess there won't be any little princes and princesses, from the look of it!" Aisha yelled to Zoey, clapping with the rest of them.

Lucas came straight over, smiling now as if the burden of the world had just been lifted from his shoulders. "It's over, it's over. I've done my little thing for school spirit. Jeez, I can't slow dance worth spit."

"You looked good," Aisha said, making a gagging sound.

"No, don't start with me, Aisha." Lucas shook his finger at her. "I still think you're the one who started this by nominating me."

The music stayed slow, and couples were drifting around the floor again, locked in embraces. "Come on, Lucas," Zoey said. "If you can dance like a dork with Louise, you can dance like a dork with me."

"I'll just go and drink punch with the pathetic, dateless people," Aisha said good-naturedly.

Lucas took Zoey in his arms. She laid her head on his shoulder. It felt very, very good to be close to him like this. Seeing him with another girl had driven that feeling home to her.

She looked across the room and saw Jake standing stiffly beside Claire, staring into blank space.

It was funny the way emotional bonds were forged, seeming stronger than any steel at the time, and then were broken, leaving two people who had shared almost everything feeling like strangers.

Today she had her arms around Lucas. Once it would have been Jake. Today she would swear that nothing could ever drive her from Lucas. But once she had felt just that same way about Jake.

There were so many ways for things to go wrong, it seemed. And so few chances that they would all go right. She was glad when Lucas slowly turned her away so that she could no longer see Jake and be reminded that even the things that felt so perfect, like the feel of being weightless in Lucas's arms, could someday end.

Then she saw Nina standing with Benjamin. They were holding hands, looking uncomfortable, maybe a little giddy, but holding hands. Sort of the way Zoey had taught Nina.

Zoey smiled. Things didn't always turn out badly.

Benjamin could feel the pulse in Nina's wrist. Her heart was racing. Fear or excitement or both. But then, his own pulse was speeding, too. Nina's nervousness must be catching.

"I have to go to the place," Nina said.

"The *place*? You mean, what, the supermarket?"

"Very cute. The ladies' room. I was trying to be delicate."

"As long as you wash your hands afterward."

"You want me to park you somewhere?" Nina suggested. "Aisha's over by the food."

"Cool." Benjamin took her arm and fell in step

191

with her. Here, in an environment this unstructured, he was genuinely blind. You couldn't use step-counting to get around a big crowded room filled with rowdy kids. "So, Aisha with the food. Is she fat or anything? You know, so I don't make some insensitive remark?"

"Yes," Nina said. "Aisha must be, oh, two, two hundred fifty pounds. Somewhere in there. Maybe three hundred."

Benjamin laughed. Obviously Nina was lying. But then, he had set her up. He knew perfectly well what Aisha looked like, having had her described several times over the years. Of course, Nina knew that, too.

Even as nervous and preoccupied and scared as she was, Nina was still right there, always sharp and on top of things. There were times when they could have almost been some old-time comedy team who had worked together for so many years, they'd become two halves of the same brain.

But something was happening. Something different. She wasn't plain old Nina to him right now. The way she smelled, the sound of her voice, the softness of her hand on his, the silkiness of her hair brushing against his cheek when she leaned close to talk to him. It was making his heart race.

"Hey, Ben." Aisha's voice.

Nina moved away. "I'll be right back unless the line is really long."

"What's up, Aisha?" he asked, immediately missing the warmth of Nina's hand.

Silence. She had probably shrugged. Then, "Oh, sorry. Not much."

"Too bad Christopher couldn't be here, huh?"

Now she was nodding.

"Well, soon, right? You think you two will get

back together after he gets out of the hospital?'' He felt uncomfortable making small talk about someone else's relationship, but it was either that or stand there like a redwood.

"I haven't really thought about it," Aisha said. "I mean, I don't know that this has really changed anything basic. But I know I don't feel like this is the time to be pushing the issue. You know?"

"Sure. Wait till he's healthy. Then bust him."

"Mostly it was miscommunication," she said, sounding thoughtful. "I mean, we barely knew each other as people before we got involved. I didn't know how he felt about certain things."

Benjamin nodded sagely. "It's good to get to know someone first, I guess."

"Yeah, well, you people of the male persuasion don't usually want to wait around for friendship to develop first," Aisha said darkly. "You guys seem to think the order should be sex first. Everything else second."

"Guys. We're such pigs," Benjamin said. "So, you want to have sex?"

"Very funny," Aisha said tolerantly. "Are you having a good time with Nina?"

"I always have a good time with Nina."

"Yeah, but this is a different kind of good time, isn't it?"

Benjamin squirmed a little uncomfortably. "Not really."

"You were holding hands."

"Uh-huh."

"And you were dancing."

"We're at a dance. What are we supposed to do? Juggle chain saws?"

"You two look good together," Aisha said. "Sort

193

of like if Christian Slater and Claire Danes were going out. Cool, but not phony."

Benjamin was ashamed to feel gratified by that comment. "Look, we're just friends at a dance together. Don't make a big thing out of it. We've been friends for a long time."

"You never held her hand before. I mean, you and I are friends, right? We're at a dance together, right? You and I are not holding hands."

Benjamin sighed irritably. "Is there any punch or cookies or anything left?"

"You know, you're blushing."

"No I'm not."

"All I'm saying is, Nina is a *hand-holding* type of friend. She's a *dance-with* type of friend. This is all new. She didn't use to be in either of those categories."

"Things change," Benjamin admitted.

"Don't get pissed off about it. Jeez, Benjamin, this is the way it should be. It's what I was just saying. First you're friends, then the other things. Very mature."

Were there those other things? Benjamin wondered. But then, hadn't he wanted to hold her hand? He clenched and unclenched his hand unconsciously. Yes. He had enjoyed holding her hand.

And dancing? Yes, he'd liked that, too.

And there was no one whose company he enjoyed more.

Still, that didn't make it anything more than friendship, really. Did it?

"Friendship," he muttered aloud, momentarily forgetting about Aisha. How did you know when friendship had become something more? How would he know if and when he crossed that line in his feelings for Nina?

"What did you say?" Aisha asked.

He shook his head. "Nothing. I was just mumbling."

"Hey, Nina," Aisha said.

Nina said something, but a group of girls nearby had burst out into a prolonged explosion of giggling.

"What?" he yelled.

She put her mouth close to his ear. He could smell her shampoo, her perfume. Her. Nina's breath tickled his ear. He realized his heart was beating fast again. And then he realized he desperately wanted her to stay just as near as she was.

His reaction almost made him laugh. So. Maybe the line had already been crossed without his noticing it.

"I said, I'm back," Nina said.

"I'm glad," he said.

It's time, Claire told herself heavily. Time to do what she had come here tonight to do.

"Come on, Jake," she said softly, taking his hand.

"We've already danced a couple times," Jake said stiffly.

"I know. I want to dance this dance."

Jake sighed. "Well, I owe you, don't I?" he said sarcastically. "How can I say no?"

"One last dance, Jake. The very last."

She drew him with her onto the floor. For a big guy he danced well, with more grace than would be expected of a football player. Claire enjoyed the hard, washboard feel of his stomach and chest, the ridged muscles of his back, even though they were tense, as they had been all night.

He was fighting his feeling for her. She could see

it in his eyes, and hear it in the strain of his voice.

"Jake, Jake," she said wearily. "We have not been a lucky couple, have we?"

He shrugged his answer.

"It's enough to make me believe in fate. And I guess there's no fighting fate, is there?"

Again he didn't answer.

"For the record, Jake, I think you are an amazing, decent, sweet guy. One of a kind. I'm sorry about all the conflict I've caused in your life, and the pain."

He met her gaze for almost the first time that night. He looked troubled.

"But this is it," Claire said. "This has to be the end. It's either me or Wade. One of us had to lose and . . ." She took a deep breath. ". . . he's already lost all he could."

"Claire—"

"No, don't, all right?" she said harshly. "This is hard enough. I really do care for you, and I know you care for me, so don't make me any sadder by saying it. There's just too much history between us. And to tell you the truth, I'm not a person who can go around for long feeling guilty. I'm sorry about what happened two years ago. I'm sorry you can't deal with this without trying to destroy yourself. But you can't. Which leaves only one solution."

His arms tightened around her, holding her close. She pressed her cheek against his shoulder and blotted her tears on his shirt.

He took her face with his hand and forced her to look at him. He kissed her for a long, still moment.

Then she took another deep breath. She let the emotion run out of her, turning her thoughts away. She thought of her widow's walk. She thought of how much she liked to be up there, watching the lightning illuminate the darkness, watching snow drift down to settle on the little town below.

She had always been able to do what she had to. And now she pulled away, leaving the warmth of Jake's arms. She turned and, with dry eyes, walked away.

Nina had been feeling increasingly uncomfortable since the band had eased into all slow songs. She hadn't danced slow with Benjamin yet. And now the entire room, at least all the people who had dates, seemed to have settled into slow-motion making out, barely acknowledging the music anymore, oblivious to the looks of others around them.

Nina set down the glass of soda.

"Are you ready for me to step on your feet some more?" Benjamin asked.

"Um, how about if we go outside for a minute. I think it's stuffy in here. No air. Don't you want to?"

"Sure. Lead on."

She led him around the perimeter of the dance floor, noticing again the way whispers seemed to follow them. She was painfully aware of the discomfort she felt, as all the feelings she'd not yet learned to bury rose to the surface.

She reached the door and pushed open the bar. A blast of chill air slapped her. Outside, more couples were making out along the wall. A group of guys and girls was walking slowly around the building, drinking from beers concealed in their coat pockets, moving to stay out of range of the chaperons. In the nearby parking lot a half-dozen guys seemed to be egging each other on to a fight. A teacher was running to intervene.

"Full moon," Nina said, automatically describing the things Benjamin couldn't see.

"A faint smell of pot, beer, and car exhaust," Benjamin said with a smile.

"I wouldn't be surprised," Nina said. She rubbed her arms with her hands, trying to stay warm.

"Are you okay?" Benjamin asked.

Nina sighed. "Yeah. I'm okay."

"That wasn't very convincing."

"I guess it wasn't," she acknowledged. "I guess I'm just not used to all this."

"What aren't you used to? The bad music? The cheap vodka someone dumped in the punch?"

"Ahh," Nina groaned, covering her face with her hands. "I'm such a dweeb. Why do you even want to go out with me? God. I'm pathetic. My hands are sweating and my heart's going like a scared rabbit's, and I feel like I'm ready to hurl."

Benjamin laughed. "Don't do *that*. Or at least, aim away from me."

"You don't understand, Benjamin."

"I'm making you sick?"

"It's not really very funny," Nina said, feeling defeated and depressed. Here it was at last—the moment when she ruined everything. The final scenario.

"I never thought I'd hear you saying something wasn't funny," Benjamin said.

"It's pathetic, how about that? *I'm* pathetic."

"No, you're not. I like you a lot, Nina. And I have very good taste. I would never like someone who was pathetic. What is this about?"

Nina groaned again in frustration and anger. "It's about the way I felt inside when you asked me to slow dance just now. I know it's dumb. I know it's *you*, not . . . someone else. And I know it's *now*, not five

198

years ago. And I'm sixteen, not a little kid anymore. But these feelings . . .''

Benjamin waited patiently for her to go on, but she couldn't. She was choking from the lump in her throat. Tears had begun to fall down her cheeks. She was ruining it, as she'd known she would. Benjamin would be sweet and understanding, but it would still be the end.

The end, after all the time she had wanted for this night to come.

"Nina, we don't have to slow dance. We don't have to kiss or anything like that."

Nina laughed bitterly. "Yeah, I'll bet kissing me would be the top thing on your list right now. Right behind getting the hell out of here and away from me."

"At the risk of making you feel even more panicky, Nina, I do want to kiss you. I've wanted to kiss you all night. All night I've felt like, jeez, I really am blind not to have realized—" He shrugged and sucked in a deep breath. "It's just that there you were, all the time, and I never realized it."

Nina bit her knuckle till she could taste blood. He was saying the things she'd hoped for years to hear him say. But at the same time she felt like running away, running all the way back to the ferry and hiding in her room. Her stomach was in knots. It wouldn't work. It never would.

"But, you know, we really can just go back inside and hang out," Benjamin said.

"Yeah," Nina managed. "Okay."

She moved to where he could take her arm. Out here in a dirt field with no landmarks to navigate by, he was almost helpless. She led him back to the door and pulled it open. Music and warmth came billowing out.

Nina stopped. A panicky, giddy, reckless feeling had taken hold of her. She let the door handle go and swung around. She darted her face forward, eyes closed, and quickly kissed Benjamin's mouth.

Only he moved and she missed his mouth.

A slow smile spread across Benjamin's face. "Feel better? Now that you've kissed my nose?"

A terrible, ghastly embarrassment flooded Nina's brain. She had kissed him on the nose. The big moment of her entire life and she had kissed him on the nose. This was not part of any scenario.

But another part of her could not help but acknowledge that it *was* funny.

"I've always really liked your nose," she said. Then she broke up in giggles.

"How about we try again? This time I'll stay still."

Nina's giggles died away. She took a deep breath, and then another. His hand had touched her bare shoulder and from there traveled to her cheek.

He was very close now, and she knew that soon the memories would rise to destroy this fragile moment.

She closed her eyes, trembling.

She felt a softness on her lips.

She felt the warmth of his breath. The muscles in his back and shoulders as her arms went around him. The luxurious, glowing heat that spread through her, banishing the chill of the Maine night.

Nina kissed him back.

And she did not hurl.

Making Out:
Claire Gets Caught

Dating.   Kissing.   Pressure.   What else could it be but
book 5?

First **Zoey** fooled around with **Lucas** and **Jake**
found out. Then **Claire** wanted **Jake,** so she broke
up with **Ben** but ended up alone. Now **Claire** has
a scheme to get **Jake** back. It's foolproof—unless...

Claire
Gets
Caught.